DOC SAVAGE'S AMAZING CREW

William Harper Littlejohn, the bespectacled scientist who was the world's greatest living expert on geology and archaeology.

Colonel John Renwick, "Renny," his favorite sport was pounding his massive fists through heavy, paneled doors.

Lieutenant Colonel Andrew Blodgett Mayfair, "Monk," only a few inches over five feet tall, and yet over 260 pounds. His brutish exterior concealed the mind of a great scientist.

Major Thomas J. Roberts, "Long Tom," was the physical weakling of the crowd, but a genius at electricity.

Brigadier General Theodore Marley Brooks, slender and waspy, he was never without his ominous, black sword cane.

WITH THEIR LEADER, THEY WOULD GO ANYWHERE, FIGHT ANYONE, DARE EVERYTHING—SEEKING EXCITEMENT AND PERILOUS ADVENTURE!

About Doc Savage:

DOC SAVAGE: HIS APOCALYPTIC LIFE
by Philip José Farmer

THE
SPOOK LEGION

A DOC SAVAGE ADVENTURE

BY KENNETH ROBESON

BANTAM BOOKS
TORONTO · NEW YORK · LONDON

THE SPOOK LEGION

*A Bantam Book / published by arrangement with
The Condé Nast Publications Inc.*

PRINTING HISTORY

Originally published in DOC SAVAGE *Magazine April 1935*
Bantam edition / March 1967

2nd printing ...... July 1967	*4th printing .... October 1968*
3rd printing .... January 1968	*5th printing ..... August 1977*

ISBN 0–553–11318–6

Published simultaneously in the United States and Canada

*Bantam Books are published by Bantam Books, Inc. Its trade-
mark, consisting of the words "Bantam Books" and the por-
trayal of a bantam, is registered in the United States Patent
Office and in other countries. Marca Registrada. Bantam
Books, Inc., 666 Fifth Avenue, New York, New York 10019.*

THE SPOOK LEGION

Chapter 1

THE FIRST SPOOK

LEO BELL was a counter clerk in a Boston telegraph office. Leo was level-headed. He certainly did not believe in spooks. At least, he did not believe in spooks at precisely ten o'clock at night, as he moved behind the counter straightening the books of message blanks.

At five minutes past ten Leo's disbelief in spooks received a rude jarring.

It happened that Leo Bell was an ambitious young man who had studied the finer points of selling, so, of course, he knew the importance of making things convenient for a customer, even the small things. It was Leo's habit to place three or four books of message blanks on the counter top so that prospective senders of telegrams had merely to step up and start writing.

As he went along tidying the counter, Leo examined each of these books, because careless customers sometimes went off and left scribbling on them. At this particular examination, all of the blanks were clean and fresh, showing unmarked sheets. Leo was sure of that. He remembered it particularly.

Leo stood at the end of the counter and waited for a customer. None came in. Leo was positive of that, also. No one even passed on the street outside. It was very quiet.

Then the wastebasket upset.

The wastebasket was not placed exactly where it should have been—near the writing table—but was out about a yard from the table. It upset noisily. Trash fell out.

Leo Bell leaned over the counter and his eyes popped. He licked his lips. Then he rubbed a hand over his eyes. Finally, he walked around the counter. He thought a cat or a dog might have gotten into the wastebasket. But there was no cat or dog.

Leo straightened the basket, then stood and scratched his head, trying to decide what had overturned the basket, and failing to reach any satisfactory conclusion, he moved over to the counter. There, he got his next shock.

The telegraph blanks there had borne no writing when he

1

arranged them a moment before. But one now bore a message printed in heavy but somewhat uncertain strokes. It read:

DOC SAVAGE
NEW YORK CITY
MATTER OF VITAL DANGER TO THOUSANDS MERITS YOUR ATTENTION STOP PLEASE BOARD BOSTON TO NEW YORK PASSENGER PLANE OF EXCELSIOR AIRWAYS AT NOON TO-MORROW STOP GET ABOARD IN BOSTON STOP SUGGEST YOU USE DISGUISE AND BE PREPARED FOR HIDEOUS AND AMAZING EXPERIENCE   A N ONYMOUS

(1440 Powder Road)

Leo Bell stared at the message, noting that it was marked to be sent collect at destination. He was dumfounded. He felt as if cold water had trickled unexpectedly down the back of his neck. He eyed the address on the message and shook his head, because he knew, from past experience, that a telegram addressed to one man in a city as large as New York had very little chance of being delivered.

Leo carried the message back to the night manager.

"I have here a straight telegram addressed to Doc Savage in New York City," he told the night manager. "I think we should get a better address."

"Where have you been all your life?" demanded the manager.

"Huh?" Leo blinked.

"I thought everybody had heard of Doc Savage," said the other.

LEO asked, "Who is this Doc Savage?"

The night manager opened his mouth as if to speak, but did not.

"Wait," he said. "I'll show you something."

The night manager walked to his desk in the rear. The night manager was a studious individual. There was a large book open on his desk. The counter clerk knew this book was a late work outlining in brief the discoveries of scientists during the past ten years or so. The night manager was interested in different branches of science. He riffled through the pages, and opened them to the section marked, "Light."

"Read this," he advised, and pointed out a paragraph.

Some of the most advanced study of the dispersion

of doubly refracting and naturally gyrating substances has been conducted by Clark Savage, Jr., (better known as Doc Savage).

Leo Bell asked, "What are naturally gyrating and doubly refracting substances?"

"Never mind," said the night manager.

He opened the book at another section marked, "Chemistry," and said, "Read this."

Great impetus has been given colorimetric analysis by recent work of Doc Savage.

Before Leo could speak, the night manager turned to another part of the book marked, "Electricity," and pointed out an item:

To Doc Savage, the field of electric science is indebted for new theories concerning velocity of propagation of electro-magnetic effects through air.

The night manager hurriedly shifted to a portion of the volume designated as dealing with "Surgery."

One of the greatest methods of recent years for the intravenous administration of hypertonic solutions in delicate brain operations is credited to Doc Savage.

Leo Bell exploded.

"*Whew!*" he gulped. "That guy Doc Savage seems to be tops at everything!"

The night manager grinned. "There's a note at the front of this book about him. It says that Doc Savage has one of the most remarkable brains of any man ever to live. It says he is a mental marvel."

They both re-read the telegram which had been found on the counter blank. Leo Bell now broached the subject of the upsetting wastebasket and the mysterious appearance of the missive, but he spoke hesitantly, and none too firmly, because the whole thing seemed ridiculous.

The night manager laughed him down.

"Somebody came in and left the message," he said. "Of course we'll send it!"

They sent it.

HALF an hour later, the telephone rang, and Leo Bell answered it. He heard the most striking voice to which he had ever listened. It was a man's voice, and even over the telephone it had impressive quality and a tone of great flexibility and power under careful restraint. There was something compelling about the voice.

"This is Doc Savage speaking from New York City," the voice said. "A telegram to me was filed from your office tonight, was it not?"

So gripping was the unusual voice that Leo Bell had to swallow twice to loosen his own vocal cords.

"Yes, sir," he said.

"Will you describe the sender, please," Doc Savage requested over the telephone.

"I c-can't," Leo Bell stuttered. It was the first time he had stuttered in years.

"Why not?" queried the unusual voice.

The mysterious circumstances surrounding the appearance of the message then came out. Doc Savage heard it through without comment, then advised, "There is probably no A. N. Onymous listed in your directory."

Leo Bell looked in the directory.

"No," he said. "There is not."

"The name was the result of a trick writing of the word 'anonymous,'" Doc pointed out. "The dictionary defines an anonymous work as one of unknown authorship, which seems to fit this case. Was there an address of sender given on the message?"

"There was."

"What was it?"

"1440 Powder Road," said Leo Bell, after consulting the message.

"There is no such address in Boston," Doc Savage said, and hung up.

Leo blinked dazedly after the connection was broken, wondering how Doc Savage had known the address was a fake —and it was indeed false. Leo ascertained a moment later, upon consulting the street directory. There was no such number on Powder Road.

Leo wondered vaguely if Doc Savage did not know as much about Boston as he did about the different branches of science. Leo would have been surprised.

The two employees in the telegraph office discussed the happening through the remainder of their tour of duty. It seemed as if something smacking of high adventure had touched them briefly, and they rather liked the manner in which it spiced their humdrum lives.

They would have liked more of it. But this was, fortunately, or unfortunately, as near as they were to come to the chain of horror and mystery which followed the sending of the strange message.

The affair really got under way the next day at noon.

THE Excelsior Airways was among the most modern lines serving the east coast of the United States. Their planes were huge tri-motored jobs carrying a pilot, co-pilot and a stewardess in the crew.

The seats were comfortable, and each bore a number, for it was customary for passengers to make seat reservations in advance. The passengers who got aboard were prosperous-looking individuals, business persons obviously—with one exception.

The fat man was not the one exception. There was nothing particularly outstanding about him. He was neither larger nor smaller than the average portly man. His gray suit was neat, well-tailored. The only thing which characterized him at all was the black felt hat which he wore, and his white-gold-rimmed spectacles which he adjusted from time to time as if they were not comfortable.

This fat man presented two tickets. These called for seats located one behind the other. The fat man walked slowly down the aisle and took the rearmost of the two seats which his tickets called for.

If any one noticed there was something just a bit strange in that, they gave no sign.

And if there was nothing exceptional about the appearance of the fat man, there was a great deal out of the ordinary about the last passenger to enter the ship. The size of this man was tremendous. He had to bend over much more than any one else as he came down the plane aisle.

Nor was his great size the least of the man's marked qualities. His face was something with which to frighten infants. It was scarred in fearsome fashion. The ears were thickened, tufted with welts. One of the eyes drooped almost shut. Over the brows, there were rolls of gristle which might have been put there by much pounding. When the man opened his mouth, he showed numerous gold teeth.

The passengers looked at him curiously. The mark of the man's trade was unmistakable. He was a prize-fighter.

The pugilistic-appearing individual lurched down the aisle, came to the vacant seat ahead of the fat man, looked around, saw the closing of the plane door to indicate no more passengers were expected, and started to take the empty seat.

"No, no!" the fat man squawled.

He leaped to his feet, gave the scarred giant a lusty shove, and looked very belligerent.

The other kept his balance with the ease of a man who might have received many lusty belts in the squared ring.

"Whatsa idea?" he growled.

He had a voice fully as pleasant as the sound of a heavy box being dragged over a concrete floor.

"I reserved this seat and paid for it!" snapped the fat man.

The prizefighter scowled. His scarred face was terrible. He gave the appearance of being but little less dangerous than an angry lion, and he seemed on the point of doing violence to the other. But finally, when the hostess approached and indicated the seat which he had paid for was in the rear, but on the side of the plane which would be in the sun, he shrugged.

"You needn't have been tough about it!" he rasped to the fat man, and padded back to his rear seat.

The plane took off without more incident. To all appearances, there was to be no more excitement during the flight. But appearances are deceptive.

IT was near New York that one of the passengers forward reached up and jerked open the window beside his seat. No doubt he wanted to thrust his head out and stare at the skyscrapers of Manhattan, which were coming into view ahead and below.

As a result of the window being opened, a strong wind whipped into the plane cabin.

Swept by the gale, a square of paper appeared over the back of the empty seat in front of the fat man. It slapped into the face of the fat man. Startled, he grabbed at it, and securing it, naturally glanced at it.

The results of that one look at the paper which had been blown over the back of the empty chair were surprising. The fat man lifted slightly in his seat, as if his leg muscles had tensed. His mouth came open and round; his eyes grew equally round. He was naturally a florid man, and it was distinctly noticeable that he became pale. Suddenly he sagged back in the chair as if some nerve cord had been cut.

He sat there for some time. Then he reached under his coat, thrust a hand beneath the left armpit and brought out a stubby but deadly-looking revolver. Simultaneously, he wrenched at his hip pocket and produced a handkerchief. He wrapped the handkerchief around the muzzle of the gun as he stood up.

He leaned over the back of the empty seat in front of him. There was an expression of wild desperation on his features.

His gun went off three times, as rapidly as he could pull the trigger. The reports were loud.

In the middle of the shooting, a shriek piped out. It was an eerie, hideous shriek, a sound which held the rasp of death.

The fat man sat down and wrapped both arms over his head and face. The way he did this was very strange.

Then the voice sounded. It was a strangled voice, one which was labored, gurgling, and hardly understandable. It said four words—really two pairs of words with a slight pause between the first pair and the second. Just where the words came from, it was impossible to say. The fat man had his mouth covered with his arms. The other passengers were watching the fat man and not each other. But almost every one heard the words, which sounded above the uproar.

"Doc Savage—be careful!"

Chapter 2

NUT?

THE average American lives in a high-pressure world where things happen with rapidity. He is not inclined to become wildly excited about an occurrence which does not menace him directly.

These plane passengers were no exceptions. They merely looked around. Those farthest away stood up. Nobody screamed. Nobody yelled.

The stewardess went forward and said something to the two men in the control compartment. The assistant pilot left his seat, came back and confronted the fat man with the revolver.

"What's the idea, brother?" he demanded.

The man with the gun moistened his lips, then reached up and absently adjusted his black felt hat.

"I'm terribly sorry," he said.

The co-pilot did not seem impressed, but repeated, "What was the idea?"

The plump man became glib.

"I am an actor," he said. "I was mentally rehearsing a scene from my new show. My enthusiasm got the better of me, and before I realized this was no place for such a thing, I had leaped up and reënacted a bit from my part."

The fat man was still standing up, and he absently reached around and stowed his handkerchief in a hip pocket. The paper which had blown over the back of the empty seat was still in the hand which held the handkerchief.

The man carefully stowed the paper in an inner pocket.

The assistant pilot whipped out a hand suddenly and seized the other's gun before he could resist.

"You might have shot somebody," he said angrily.

The portly man rolled his eyes, then fixed them downward at the empty seat. Perspiration beads came out from under the band of his black hat.

"I fired blank cartridges," he said.

The associate pilot broke open the gun, ejected the cartridges, and three empties and two slugs came out. With a finger, he indicated the leaden pellets in the two unfired cartridges.

"This don't look like it," he said.

"The first three were blanks!" the plump man gulped.

"Yeah?" The flier scowled. "I'll see about that. The bullets should have hit somewhere."

He leaned over, as if to get into the empty seat and hunt for bullet holes.

The fat man did a surprising thing. He leaped back, threw out his arms dramatically and began to speak in a stagelike voice.

"The mortal moon hath her eclipse endured," he intoned. "And the sad augurs mock their own presage. Incertainties now crown themselves assured, and peace——"

The associate pilot straightened.

"What the hell?" he demanded.

"Shakespeare," declared the plump man. "The supreme dramatist, my good fellow. The supreme dramatist! And a very good friend he was indeed." The man winked and crossed two fingers. "He and I were like that."

The pilot smiled slightly, and his weather-beaten features assumed a knowing look. He winked at the other passengers, then dropped an arm over the fat man's shoulder.

"So you and Shakespeare were buddies," he said, with the manner of one agreeing with a person he considers insane. "Tell me about it, mister. I've always wanted to meet some one who knew Shakespeare."

"Shakespeare was the supreme dramatist," said the fat man. "Knowing him was a pleasure, a supreme pleasure. Indeed it was!"

"Sure, sure," said the pilot.

The aviator thrust the portly one down in his seat, then sat on the chair arm and encouraged him to talk ramblingly of Shakespeare, who had been dead hundreds of years. The plane swung down toward the landing field.

The passengers had been interested in the little drama. Two or three had crowded close, among these the big fellow who looked like a prizefighter. He had looked closely at the empty seat into which the gun had been discharged.

There were no holes or tears in the seat where a bullet might have struck.

The prizefighter individual went back to his seat. Seated in such a position that no one could see his hands, he opened one hand and examined the object which it held. This was the fat man's handkerchief, the one which had been wrapped around the gun muzzle. It had been filched from the owner with consummate cleverness.

There were holes in the handkerchief, undoubtedly holes made by leaden bullets ripping through.

THE plane landed without event, and the portly man arose to get his baggage and disembark with the rest of the passengers. But the co-pilot grasped his arm firmly and requested, "Please wait."

The plump man's next words were not nearly as inane as his earlier ramblings.

"What for?" he demanded.

"Shakespeare wants to see you," said the flier.

It looked as if the portly one was on the point of venting an explosive, "Hell!" but he did not. Instead, he stated, "Shakespeare has been dead a long time."

"Well, you'd better talk to this fellow who says he is Shakespeare," said the assistant pilot, and went forward to consult with the airport operations manager.

They discussed the fat man and the shots.

"He's daffy," said the co-pilot. "Something ought to be done about a guy like that running around with a gun. He'll kill somebody."

"Put him in a car and take him to the police station," suggested the manager.

"Good idea," agreed the co-pilot.

"The pilot will help you," added the manager.

There were two observers to this conference, neither of whom was close enough to overhear. The fat man was one, standing and fumbling his black hat uncertainly. The prizefighter individual was another, although he looked on in a fashion calculated not to arouse suspicion. He was ostensibly fumbling over his baggage.

The plane had emptied by now, and mechanics had appeared to wheel it into a hangar. One of them drove a small caterpillar tractor, which was hitched to the ship and pulled it toward the hangar.

The pilot and co-pilot approached the fat man.

"We're going to take you to this guy who claims to be Shakespeare," said the pilot.

The plump fellow put a very serious look under the black hat.

"The man is an imposter!" he declared loudly. "He cannot be Shakespeare, because *I* am Shakespeare!"

The instant he got that out, the man spun and leaped wildly in the direction of the operations office. The abruptness of his move took the pilot and his assistant by surprise. By the time they started in pursuit, their quarry was already passing through the operations office door. He slammed the panel. The spring lock clicked.

Pilot and co-pilot hit the door with their shoulders. It held. They bounced back, looked at each other.

"He's sure bats!" said the pilot.

Inside, the fat man made a silent snarl when he heard that. His face had been benign, a bit vacuous. The snarl turned it into the visage of an animal.

He fanned a glance around the room. There was a desk, a typewriter. He leaped to the typewriter, seized it and used it as a clumsy club, and with one driving blow, smashed glass and metal crosspieces from a window in the rear wall. The aperture was hardly ample to pass his plump frame, and he struck again, so violently that his black hat fell off. Then he started to jump through.

His eyes lighted on a small group of men standing a short distance away. He waved his arms and caught their attention.

The fat man now made a remarkable series of gestures with his hands. These gestures were small—such casual movements as might be made unthinkingly by a man who was merely idling time away. He rubbed thumb and forefinger together. He made various kinds of fists. He drummed soundlessly with his fingers.

All of these small gestures were made with lightning speed, and the group of men whom the fat fellow had sighted saw them, and when they were finished, one went through the motion of adjusting his right coat sleeve slightly.

The fat man's manner showed that the sleeve adjusting was a signal that his other pantomiming had been understood.

The fat man now turned, picked up his black hat, put it on, went over to a mirror and tried three or four grins before he got one which was particularly silly. With it fixed on his face, he opened the door and admitted the excited pilot and his assistant.

"What on earth has so excited you fellows?" he demanded calmly.

THE men to whom the fat individual had signaled were no longer standing inactively. They had moved at a fast walk toward the hangar where the passenger plane had been hauled. The noisy little caterpillar tractor was still attached to the plane, and three field attendants were assisting in storing the air giant.

The attendants stared in surprise at the group to whom the fat man had signaled. The men had stalked into the hangar without speaking.

There were six men in the group. They ranged from a young fellow who looked as if he might be a high school student to a white-haired individual who looked as if he were past sixty. None of them wore flashy clothing, but all were neat. Neither would any of them attract attention because of their garb. They might have been a party of conservatively dressed business people. It was certain that all of their faces were above the average in intelligence.

"What do you want?" demanded one of the airport flunkies.

One of the six strangers coughed twice. It was obviously a signal—for all six men drew revolvers and pistols of various sizes and calibres.

"Silence," said the one who had coughed. "We want a lot of it, too!"

The attendant stuttered, "W-w-what's t-t-the idea?"

"Turn around," directed the spokesman. "Stand with your backs to us."

The attendants complied, which was obviously the sensible thing to do.

Two of the six nice-looking strangers kept the attendants covered while the other four went to the plane, opened the cabin door and scrambled inside. The plane, being large and high, could not be surveyed from the level of the hangar floor. One of the attendants, turning his head, could not see what the four in the ship were doing.

Another of the attendants did not waste more than a single glance on the ship, then shifted his attention to a row of oil drums a few feet from where he stood, a row three drums thick and almost as high as his own belt, and extending several yards to a small side door used by the mechanics. This door was open.

One of the four strangers in the plane all but fell out of the cabin door. He was highly perturbed.

"It ain't here!" he said shrilly.

"But did you look in the seat?" squawled the spokesman.

"Yeah," said the other. "We went all over the ship. We even got down on our hands and knees and felt around."

The spokesman was the nice-looking old man with the white hair. He began to curse. He stopped quickly, however, and spun and grabbed one of the attendants.

"That plane door was closed when we got here," he snapped. "Was it open at any time while you were hauling the plane from in front of the operations office?"

"I d-don't k-know," stuttered the grease-monkey.

One of the nice-looking men said, "Damn it, anyhow! The door was open when the passengers got out. That was enough!"

At this point, the attendant who had been looking at the oil drums decided this was his chance. He gave a great leap, sailed over the drums, landed in their shelter and scuttled for the door.

The men with the guns yelled at him. They fired, but their bullets only made oil leak from the drums.

The attendant got outside through the door, slammed it, secured the hasp fastening, then ran away as fast as he could.

THE shots threw the airport into an uproar. Two men loading mail into a postal service truck drew their guns and took shelter behind their vehicle.

The group of nice-looking men came racing from the hangar. The mail guards yelled at them to stop, and were promptly shot at. They fired back. A pitched battle ensued, with the raiders retreating toward two sedans which were parked on the airport road.

They reached the machines, dived inside and drove off at high speed. The mail truck tried to pursue, but its tires were promptly punctured with bullets.

There was much running and shouting, but the pilot of the Boston plane and his assistant kept a tight grip on their fat prisoner. The latter was now talking quite rationally and insisting he had never claimed to be Shakespeare.

After some delay, a plane took the air to scout for the two fleeing sedans.

The burly individual who looked like a prizefighter—the

same who had been a passenger in the plane—was still at the airport. As a matter of fact, it was he who suggested that a plane be sent up in search for the sedans.

He had been observing proceedings more closely than any one suspected. But he remained in the background, and no one paid him particular attention, except to give his unusual appearance a second scrutiny.

Two other individuals were not receiving much attention. These gentlemen had not even put themselves in marked evidence. They were in a car parked on the large lot reserved for spectators at the airport.

The machine was small, unobtrusive. Only a very close scrutiny would have shown that its motor was not the one provided by the manufacturer, but one with nearly three times as much power, and that the windows were of thick bulletproof glass and the body of armor steel.

The two men sat slumped down in their seats. From time to time they pressed small but powerful binoculars to their eyes. In each case, the glasses were focused on the burly man who had the appearance of a pugilist.

The pilot and his assistant were arguing with the fat man.

"I certainly cannot recall insisting I was Shakespeare," asserted the latter. "Nor do I remember firing a revolver in your plane."

"Maybe we're wrong," the pilot said.

The fat man moistened his lips, looked indecisive, then shrugged elaborately.

"I guess I will have to tell you men my weakness," he said.

The pilot looked interested. "What do you mean?"

"I must have been airsick," said the fat man. "I have a peculiar ailment. When I become airsick or seasick, I grow slightly demented. Once, when crossing the Atlantic, I was unbalanced the whole way over."

"Hm-m-m." The pilot did not seem very impressed.

"I hope you two men are not going to embarrass me by turning me over to the police," the plump man said anxiously.

With a noisy whoop from its exhaust stacks, the plane which had taken off to search for the two sedans came in and landed. The pilot got out and reported that he had found the two cars, but that, by flying low, he had peered inside and ascertained that they were abandoned. The group of nice-looking men had escaped.

The pilot of the Boston plane gave the fat man's arm a tug and said, "Come on."

"What are you going to do?" demanded the prisoner.

"We're going to embarrass you," said the pilot, "by turning you over to the police for observation."

THE pilot used his own car, an open touring, and he got behind the wheel, designating the task of guarding the fat man to the assistant pilot. The latter was husky, and he had a gun.

"I thought for a while that you were nuts," he advised their guest. "But now you seem all right. Just keep in mind that if you try any funny business I'm liable to blow holes in you."

"Even riding in a car makes me airsick, or seasick, or landsick, or whatever it is, sometimes," said the fat man.

"You'd better hope this is not one of the times," the other told him.

They drove out of the airport.

The prizefighter individual had been loitering, but now he came to life, striding out onto the gravel area where the cars were parked. He paused beside a machine which was empty. This was a coupé. The windows were up. The man's hand made a series of lightning-fast gestures, as if he were writing on one of the windows.

There was, however, no visible mark on the window when he walked on.

The pugilistic-looking one got into a roadster. This machine was long, sombre, a vehicle designed to escape notice, to merge unobtrusively with other traffic. On this car, too, a close examination would have shown tires filled with particularly soft sponge rubber, tires which could not be punctured readily with bullets, and an enormous motor, along with armor plate and glass which could not be penetrated by ordinary bullets.

The roadster raced out of the parking lot, the grind of its tires on the gravel almost its only sound, and speeded after the touring car bearing the two fliers and the fat man who had fired the mysterious shots in the plane.

The two men who had been waiting, and occasionally using the binoculars, in the small car, now whipped open a door of the machine and alighted.

The first to appear had an astounding physique. His height was little greater than that of a boy in his early 'teens, but he had shoulders, arms, a bull neck that a professional wrestler would have envied. His head was a nubbin with an enormous slash for a mouth and eyes like small, bright beads sunken in deep pits of gristle. Reddish hair, only slightly less coarse than rusty shingle nails, covered his frame. A stranger would not have to encounter the man in a very dark alley to think he had met a bull ape.

The second man was slender, with lean hips and an hour-glass waist. His not unhandsome face was notable for its large orator's mouth. The man was attired to sartorial perfection; his frock coat, afternoon trousers, gray vest and silk topper left nothing to be desired. The costume was set off perfectly by the slender black cane which he carried.

The man who was a fashion plate wheeled to get a small leather case from the car.

"Hurry up, Ham," the apish individual urged. He had a tiny voice which was reminiscent of a small child talking.

"Ham"—Brigadier General Theodore Marley Brooks—the dressed-up one, got the case. It was about the size of those used to carry home-movie cameras. He carried it as they ran to the coupé, on the windows of which the prizefighter individual had been seen to write—yet had left no visible traces of writing.

"Hold the lantern case, Monk," directed the dapper man.

The gorillalike "Monk"—Lieutenant Colonel Andrew Blodgett Mayfair—took the leather case. Ham manipulated the device which he had extracted, an apparatus outwardly resembling a small, old-fashioned magic lantern. He turned it on the coupé window, threw a switch on the apparatus.

The lantern itself threw no visible light. But upon the glass of the car window, lettering appeared. It was very faint, almost indistinguishable in the sunlight, a nebulous tracery of eerie, electric blue. Not without some squinting difficulty, Monk read it:

Follow and keep out of sight.

There was no signature, but the writing itself was so distinctive that it needed no signature; it was machine-perfect.

Neither Monk nor Ham commented on the manner in which the message had been brought out. Ham switched off the lantern—it was in reality a projector of "black light," or ultra-violet light which was invisible to the naked eye, but which had the property of making certain substances glow, or fluoresce.

The writing on the glass had been done with a chalk which left no visible mark but only a tracing which would glow when subjected to the ultra-violet beam.

"Things are looking up," grinned the small-voiced Monk.

"Come on, you missing link!" Ham told him unkindly.

The tone was insulting, but it seemed to make no impression on the homely Monk. They turned toward their car.

From down the road came a series of distant rapping sounds.

"Shots!" Monk squeaked.

Chapter 3

NO CHANCES

THE dapper Ham seemed to be a little faster on his feet, although the apish Monk moved with fantastic speed for one of such grotesque physique. Ham reached their car first, whipped open the door and dived for the wheel.

Out of the car came a loud, displeased squeal. There was a flurry of movement. A pig which had been in the front seat shot over onto the rear cushions. The pig had enormous ears, and as he jumped, the ears had the appearance of wings. The shote was long-legged, lean-bodied, incredibly ugly.

Monk, rumbling angrily, sent out one huge hand and closed it about the dapper Ham's throat.

"You kicked Habeas Corpus!" he gritted. "I gotta notion to see how easy your head comes off!"

Ham made croakings past the fingers constricting his throat. He tried to slug the apish Monk in the pit of the stomach, and the sound was much as if his knuckles had rapped a hard wall. He grimaced in agony, and fumbled at his black cane. The cane came apart near the handle, revealing the fact that it housed a sword with a long, razor-sharp blade. This blade was tipped for three or four inches with a sticky-looking substance.

Monk released his throat grip before the menace of the sword cane tip and dodged back. His movements were so fast that they barely could be followed with the eye.

Ham swallowed twice, then snarled, "I didn't kick that hog, but sometime I'm gonna bob his tail off right next to his ears!"

The two looked at each other with what seemed genuine, utter hate.

From down the road, the sound of more shots drifted.

"Step on it, you overdressed shyster," Monk growled.

Ham put the car in motion. His driving was expert. They were far down the road before the last of the gravel which their wheels kicked up had fallen back to the airport parking lot.

This was the same road which passed the airport, and from the city out to the airport it was wide and well paved, but here, beyond the flying field, it was narrow, rutted, flanked by high weeds and small trees. Side roads, barely more than trails, branched off at infrequent intervals toward scrawny shacks almost lost from sight in the shrubbery.

The car rocketed around a curve. Ahead, another car was cocked over into the ditch. It was the machine driven by the pilot and his assistant. Three tires were flat.

Both fliers stood alongside the machine, arms held up rigidly.

Clustered about the car were the half dozen nice-looking men who had raided the hangar. All were armed. With them was the fat man whom the two fliers had been taking to a police station.

There was no sign of the roadster bearing the individual who resembled a prizefighter.

Ham, bent over the wheel, clipped, "What'll we do?"

"Barge right in!" Monk grunted.

Ham put more weight on the accelerator. Monk grabbed door handles and cranked. It became apparent that the unusual car was fitted with two sets of glass. The second had concealed panels, which now came into view, were thicker and equipped with thin loophole slits reënforced with steel bullet deflectors.

When he had raised all of the shields, Monk dug a peculiar weapon from an armpit holster. This gun resembled an oversize automatic with a drum magazine. Its mechanism looked intricate.

Ham trod the brakes, jockeyed the wheel. Tires shrieked on the roadway, the car rocked, and finally came to a stop not many yards from the ditched touring car.

Two of the nice-looking men broke for the brush alongside the road.

"Hold it!" Monk commanded, his small voice suddenly a great howl. "Get your hands up!"

One of the men whipped up a revolver and blasted a bullet at the homely Monk.

THE slug hit the thick bulletproof glass shield with a noisy *clank* and left a spider web of fine cracks. A flattened blob, the lead fell back to the road.

The pilot leaped at the gunman, swung a fist from near his heels and knocked the man flat on his back.

"Get down!" Monk roared at him. "We can handle this!"

Monk then shifted the muzzle of his unusual gun toward the fleeing pair. The weapon emitted an ear-splitting roar, a sound not unlike the note of a gigantic bullfiddle. Beside the running pair, weeds and small shrubs upset as if cut off by an invisible scythe.

Both fugitives stopped, stunned. They had not been touched by the storm of bullets, but they were scared, knowing the weapon was a machine pistol of a type they had never before encountered.

"Get 'em up, get 'em up!" Monk squawled. "All I gotta do is make one pass and you guys are named mud!"

It was not a situation which afforded opportunity for much debate. Guns were dropped. An automatic exploded from the shock of striking the road, but its wild bullet hit no one. Hands went up.

Monk and Ham both heaved out of the car. Monk's pet pig, Habeas Corpus, followed them.

The two airmen looked somewhat dazed.

"What in the devil is this all about?" the assistant pilot demanded.

Monk menaced carelessly the nice-looking men with his machine pistol.

"Maybe they didn't like the way you were treating their friend," he said.

"They were taking him from us," said the associate flier. "They shot our tires to pieces, then jumped out in the road when we stopped. We didn't have a chance!"

"Where were you taking the fat guy?" Monk demanded.

"To a police station up this road," the other replied. "He's nuts!"

"Nuts—hell!" the other aviator interjected. "I don't think he's any more nuts than I am."

Monk grunted, "Just what's behind this?"

"Search me!" The pilot waved his arms angrily. "This fat guy ups in our plane and shoots off a gun three times into an empty seat. Then he talked like he was bats, and knew Shakespeare. He even claimed he *was* Shakespeare!"

"What about the excitement in that hangar back at the airport?" Ham put in.

The pilot gestured at the nice-looking men. "These guys raided the hanger to look into our plane. They were hunting for something that they didn't find."

"This fat man ordered them to search the plane, I think," Ham said.

"Huh?" The pilot blinked.

Ham explained: "The fat man made some kind of sign talk through the back window of the operations office. He probably told them to rescue him, too."

The fat man, unnoticed, had sidled to one of his men and

was surreptitiously dropping a hand into the fellow's pocket. He brought out a nickeled revolver.

He did not use it. Instead, he yelled out in surprised pain and the gun left his fingers. The weapon remained suspended a few inches from his hand. He grabbed at it. The gun, with absolutely nothing visible sustaining it, evaded his clutch.

Monk gaped.

"For the love of mud!" he gulped. "Spooks!"

So astounded was the homely fellow that the gang got their chance. They moved swiftly.

Monk started to swing his machine pistol around, but was tardy, and was knocked down. A lusty kick sent the super-firer into the ditch.

Ham was also disarmed and, with the fliers, forced to put up his hands.

The pig, Habeas Corpus, retreated hastily to the nearest brush clump.

"We'd better blow!" said the plump man.

There was a noise in the brush beside the road, and a huge figure appeared. It was the individual who looked like a prize-fighter. He held a shiny revolver in one scarred lump of a fist.

"I was just ready to help you birds," he said. "But I don't guess you need me. Say, what happened to that gun?"

Instinctively, all eyes sought the gun which had behaved so mysteriously. It now lay in the ditch beside the road. No one had observed just how it got there.

"Never mind the gun!" rapped the fat man. "We're leaving here!"

"We might as well ride," said the prizefighter individual.

He ran to the car in which Monk, Ham and the pig had arrived. This was obviously the only machine available for an escape, since the tires of the aviators' touring were flat. The man dived behind the wheel and reached for the key.

The fat man and the others were running toward the car, but were not yet close enough to see the pugilist as he grasped the key, and, instead of turning it, pulled it out and palmed it. Then he got out.

"Blast them birds!" he growled.

"What's wrong?" demanded the fat man.

"They took the key!" The fellow shrugged his huge shoulders. "We'll have to leg it away from here."

"Then what are we waiting on?" the fat man snapped.

They all ran into the brush beside the road.

THEY covered a hundred yards and got themselves organized so that they traveled in a string, one behind the other, taking turns at leading the procession and opening a way through the thick tangle. The plump leader dropped back beside the prizefighter.

"I never saw you before," he said. "We ought to know each other."

"It might help," agreed the pugilist.

"What's your name?"

"Bull Retz, right now," said the scarred man. "Did you go to the fights in the Boston Arena last night?"

"I rarely go to fights," said the plump man.

"Then you didn't see me," the pugilist muttered. "It's just as well. Boy, did I get bopped around!"

"You lost, eh?"

"And how!" The man blew on a scarred fist. "There was a young punk, and could he sling his dukes! Say, that guy got red pepper on his gloves somehow and after he started my eyes smarting, he hit me with everything but the water bucket! If I ever meet that punk——"

"Let it ride." The fat man adjusted his black hat. "Like I said, I never saw you before. Why'd you help us?"

"I was coming down the road," said the others. "It looked like you guys were behind the eight ball."

The eyes under the black hat brim were very curious. "And why did you help us?"

The man who said he was "Bull" Retz seemed to consider deeply.

"You looked like right guys," he said.

"Meaning what?"

The huge shoulders shrugged. "The manager and training expenses ate up the loser's share of last night's purse. I'm flat. I mooched that plane ticket off a newspaper lug who got it for nothing. So I saw you guys, and you looked like a right crowd who would return a favor."

"I see." The plump man adjusted his hat again. "You thought we would return a favor."

"Why not?" The other squinted suddenly. "Or maybe I was mistaken?"

"You don't need to beat around the bush with me," the portly man said dryly.

"O. K." The scarred face warped into a grin. "I'm flat, like I said. I thought maybe you could throw something my way."

"What are you good at?"

The scarred grin widened. "Strong-arm stuff. And I ain't too particular."

"I see," said the fat man.

They went on, and the individual who looked like a prize-fighter began to register doubt and uneasiness; finally, he turned and confronted the fat man.

"Say," he whined, "I ain't askin' much. I done you guys a turn, see? Don't I get something out of it? I don't mean that you have to pay off. Just put me next to something. You know, something where a guy can make a buck. How about it?"

"Of course," said the fat man, "we'll put you next to something."

"Something good?"

"Very good!"

They went on, and the fat man dropped back a pace, absently sinking his hands into his pockets. He brought one hand out slyly a moment later. It held a shot-filled leather blackjack which he must have secured earlier from one of the other men. He swung the blackjack suddenly, terrifically.

It seemed that the pugilist sensed the blow coming for he sank a little, taking the swing across the top of his head. But there was a loud *thud* as the sap landed, and the scarred man sagged forward on his face, quivered a little, then became limp, unmoving.

One of the nice-looking men eyed their fat chief.

"The guy might have meant all right, Telegraph," he said.

The fat "Telegraph" nodded peacefully and returned the sap to his pocket.

"We are not in a position to take chances with gentlemen whom we do not know," he murmured.

Chapter 4

THE SNATCHING GHOST

THEY did not leave the fallen form of the pugilist immediately. Telegraph bent over and pinched him soundly, but elicited no movement which would indicate returning consciousness. Then he went through the burly individual's pockets.

He brought out letters addressed to Leopold Retz in Boston, and read them, finding all had to do with matters routine to a prizefighter's training and search for further matches. There was also a bundle of newspaper clippings, which looked fresh. They were from sporting pages, and one was headed:

A TAME BULL

Bull Retz proved one thing conclusively in his match last night. As a fighter, he makes an excellent doormat.

Telegraph laughed, and went through the other clippings. "What a fight that must have been," he murmured.

"This guy seems to have been genuine," said one of the others. "Maybe we shouldn't have bopped him."

"Why not?" Telegraph demanded. "He was a stranger, wasn't he? And what saps we would be to take a stranger in. This thing is too big for mugs like this palooka."

That seemed to settle the affair—and they went on, hurrying. One of the party evidenced a knowledge of their surroundings, and before long they came out on a heavily traveled thoroughfare. They did not advance to the pavement itself, but paralleled the road for a quarter of a mile until one of the men pointed and said, "I knew it was around here somewhere."

The object he indicated was a telephone pole alongside of which stood a small booth. It was one of the telephones provided along the highway for motorists who might need emergency aid.

One of the men went to the telephone and made a call.

"One of our cars will be out here for us in half an hour," he said.

They retired into the brush to wait and to talk.

"Give us the lowdown on what happened in that plane, Telegraph," one of the men requested.

Telegraph took off his black hat and began to turn it around on one knee.

"It seemed that everything was going perfectly," he said. "I got two seats reserved in the plane, and took the rear one. Then, when we were nearing New York, some guy up in front opened a window to stick his head out and get a look or something. That made a draft, and a paper blew out of the front seat—the seat right in front of me, I mean."

One of the men lifted a hand.

"Ps-s-t!" he warned. "A guy is driving down the road in a cart. He might hear us."

They lifted up and made out the man in the cart—the cart was rickety, laden with junk, and the man was a shabby fellow whose garb advertised his calling: a junk collector.

Telegraph ceased speaking. But that did not mean his recital was interrupted. He began to make the small, unusual gestures with his hands. The movements seemed to comprise a semaphore shorthand by which rapid communication was possible. They were certainly not the system of alphabetical letters used by the deaf and dumb.

The communication in this strange fashion went on until the peddler and his cart were out of hearing, after which oral discussion resumed. The recital seemed to have progressed a good deal during the period in which they had talked with signals.

"And you say after you fired the shots, you heard a voice yell?" asked one of the men.

"Exactly!" said Telegraph.

"Was it Easeman who yelled?"

"Easeman?" Telegraph shook his head. "I don't know. I thought Easeman was dead. By all the laws, he should be dead."

One of the men shrugged. "Well, I told you what we found when we searched the plane. Exactly nothing!"

Telegraph groaned and took his head in his hands. "It's all a damned mess—and I haven't told you what really worries me."

"What?" demanded a man.

"The words that were yelled out in the plane," said Telegraph.

"What were they?"

"Doc Savage—be careful!" announced Telegraph.

For the space of a dozen seconds, no one said anything. Then one of the men, a thin fellow who looked as if his health were none too good, leaned forward. He had become quite pale.

"Listen," he gulped hoarsely, "did I get that right? Somebody mentioned Doc Savage in that plane?"

Telegraph's nod was slow. "Exactly!"

The frail man groaned audibly, sank back and mumbled, "Now I remember!"

"You remember what?" Telegraph scowled.

The frail man straightened up nervously. "Look! What do you know about this Doc Savage?"

"Just the stuff that's cropping up in the newspapers all of the time," Telegraph said. "I don't pay much attention. Doc Savage is supposed to be a combination of muscular strength and mental skill something out of the ordinary."

"But his profession," the man gasped. "You've heard of that?"

"Maybe you'd call it a profession," Telegraph said dryly. "I don't. The man goes around mixing in other people's troubles."

"He helps those whom he thinks deserve it," the other pointed out.

"From what I've heard of him, he's a big-time adventurer —a soldier of fortune," Telegraph retorted. "But what are you getting at?"

"You've heard of his five assistants—I mean the five guys who help Doc Savage?" asked the one who was patently scared.

Telegraph nodded impatiently. "I've read of them, too. Each one of them is supposed to be a specialist in a particular line. One is a chemist, another a lawyer, another an engineer, one an electrical expert and——"

"Say!" interposed another of the group. "What has all of this got to do with the fact that Doc Savage's name was yelled out in that plane? I've seen Doc Savage. I know him by sight. Once you see that guy, you'll never forget him. He wasn't on that plane."

"Shut up!" snapped the frightened one. "I'm talking about his two assistants named Monk and Ham. Monk is the chemist in his line-up, and Ham is the lawyer."

"So what?" Telegraph asked wearily.

"So didn't you ever hear of the pet pig named Habeas Corpus that this chemist, Monk, carries around with him?" demanded the other.

"Pig!" Telegraph looked stunned. "Why—those two men back there—they had a pig!"

"You said it!" the other told him. "The guy who looked like an ape was Monk. The other one, the bird with that black cane, was Ham. That's a sword cane."

Telegraph took his head in his hands. For a long minute, he said nothing.

"This is hell," he muttered finally.

"It's a fair sample," the frail man said grimly. "But when this Doc Savage catches up with us, we'll get the real thing. I've heard things about that guy."

THERE was silence while they said nothing and exchanged uneasy glances.

"Doc Savage has got a line on us," one said. "How did that happen?"

Another reached out suddenly and gripped Telegraph's arm.

"Was it Easeman who yelled out in the plane?" he demanded.

"I don't know," Telegraph said wearily. "It was a strangled voice. And I told you I thought Easeman was dead."

"How do you account for the note that blew into your face?" he was asked.

The man put his black hat on his head and unfolded the note under discussion.

"There were little boxes with writing paper, ink and a pen on the backs of the seats," he said. "This is a sheet of the paper. Here—look it over."

The men crowded their heads together to read the note. Telegraph stood up and moved away from them a few paces and kept his eyes fixed on the road. It was a busy highway. Cars passed at intervals. Telegraph came back when the men had finished reading.

"That makes it pretty plain what has happened, does it not?" he asked. "That's Easeman's handwriting, you know."

"But how'd he get the information?" one of the group questioned vacantly.

"By spying on us!" Telegraph snapped. "That's the only way he could have gotten it. Damn that fellow! He wasn't as weak as we thought. He was getting ready to gang up on us." He tapped the note angrily. "This proves it!"

"Maybe Easeman rang in Doc Savage," some one suggested.

"I've been thinking of that," Telegraph said. "It's not nice to think about. Hell's bells! Just when we thought we had things going nicely!"

"Maybe Easeman is dead after all," a man muttered hopefully.

"That would help," Telegraph agreed.

Telegraph was refolding the note slowly. Holding it between thumb and forefinger, he prepared to stow it back in his pocket. He never completed the gesture.

His mouth flew wide. A shriek ripped out. His pudgy frame convulsed. His legs drew up and an uncanny thing happened —for the space of several seconds, he seemed to be suspended entirely in mid-air, with nothing whatever supporting him. Then he collapsed heavily to the earth.

The note came out of his pocket and fluttered up vertically to a height of some six feet, opening as it arose, then the breeze seemed to catch it and the missive fluttered away, spinning over and over.

Telegraph's face was a mask of horror. He fought to regain his voice.

"Use your guns!" he shrieked.

THE men had picked up their weapons on the road after the fellow who looked like a pugilist had released them. They whipped the guns out, began shooting. Their firing was wild. They aimed at no target, but it was noticeable that they did not drive bullets into the air, or into the earth. The slugs clipped leaves, chiseled bark off trees.

Telegraph scrambled to his feet. His features were flushed, his eyes protruded. He stroked his neck.

On his neck, long purple marks were visible. At one point, the skin had been broken. Scarlet drops gathered there, loosened from their anchorage and chased each other down to stain his neat white collar. He seemed to recover his self-control.

"It's no use!" he yelled. "Stop shooting!"

The thunder of guns ceased.

"Where'd that note go?" Telegraph demanded.

A man pointed. "Over that way. The wind blew it."

"Get it!" Telegraph snapped. "Then we'll clear out of here."

Their behavior was strange. They grouped together, back to back, eyes, ears and guns alert, and moved for the spot the breeze had carried the bit of paper. Covering some yards, they began to look about with increasing anxiety.

"It's gone!" Telegraph groaned.

One of the men yelled, pointed.

"Look!" he bawled.

Fifty yards distant, a bush was swaying as if it had been disturbed. There was, however, nothing visible in the shrubbery. The men advanced, guns ready, until one, eying the ground, made a hissing sound and leveled an arm.

The earth was soft, and it bore tracks—footprints and such marks as a man might make while crawling on the ground.

"Somebody was hanging around," Telegraph grated.

They broke into a run, following the tracks. A moment later, they caught sight of a flashing motion ahead. It was a man, a giant of a figure, lunging for the shelter of a clump of trees. They all saw him.

"It's that damn prizefighter!" Telegraph snarled. "We should've finished him off!"

Two of them discharged bullets. Both, knowing they had missed, cursed.

"Spread out," commanded Telegraph. "We'll get that guy out of our hair, anyhow!"

A thin wailing sound sprang up in the distance and grew perceptibly louder. It had an unearthly quality. Telegraph and his men exchanged pained glances.

"State troopers," Telegraph said.

From near by on the road came the three musical notes of an automobile air horn. Almost immediately, the notes repeated.

"That's our car," one volunteered. "We'd better blow."

"Good idea," agreed Telegraph.

They sprinted for the road.

As they ran, the men whipped out handkerchiefs and carefully wiped finger prints from their guns. Then they threw the weapons away. They had obviously experienced difficulty with the police before and knew of the regulations against carrying firearms.

"Sure none of you left finger prints inside of your guns when you oiled them last?" Telegraph puffed. "And you wiped off the magazines of the automatics before you clipped them in?"

"Think we're amateurs?" some one grunted.

They reached their car. It was a big sedan, neither too old nor too new. A neatly dressed, pleasant-faced young man was driving. He got the doors open.

"Cops must have heard your little war," he offered. "Where d'you wanta go?"

Telegraph was the last into the car. He leaned out to grasp the door and close it.

"We'll have a talk with Easeman's daughter," he said grimly. "You know the address—Central Park West. She may have a line on her old man."

He was facing the brush patch which they had just quitted when he said that.

The sedan door slammed shut. The driver let out the clutch and clashed gears. The machine lunged away. It gathered speed rapidly, going in a direction opposite that from which came the siren noise of the State police car.

The car was not yet out of sight, nor had the police machine put in an appearance—there was a bend in the highway which hid it from view—when there was a great crashing in the brush and Monk and Ham put in an appearance. They had been running, but neither breathed heavily, an indication of good physical condition. The afternoon garb of the lawyer, Ham, was somewhat less immaculate than it had been before. He still carried his sword cane. The pig, Habeas Corpus, trailed them.

It was the shote which first located the personage who resembled a prize-fighter. The latter was standing in a brush clump, holding the compact cylinder of a telescope.

Monk and Ham ran to him. Both grinned widely, and the pig, Habeas Corpus, bounced about as if delighted beyond measure.

"Say, Doc, what's this all about?" Monk questioned.

Chapter 5

GIRL IN GREEN

THE giant with the scars, the tufted ears, the nodular hands, dropped the telescope in a pocket and wheeled back into the brush.

Out on the road, the State police car wailed along slowly, the two uniformed occupants looking for the source of the shots which must have been heard some distance away. Possibly the yelling of Telegraph's men had also been heard, and some one had put in a call for the officers.

"What about them cops?" Monk demanded.

"They would ask questions for an hour or so." The pugilistic-looking man gestured in the direction of the airport. "We have places to go."

They retreated, slowly at first, being careful to make no noise, then more swiftly. The giant with the pugilistic appearance had undergone a series of striking changes. He had straightened his hunched shoulders, and his head, which had been carried drawn down so as to thicken out the neck, was now carried normally. He seemed fully a foot taller than before. Gone also was the shuffling method of handling his feet which is a characteristic of many professional fighters.

"What started the shooting back there, Doc?" Monk asked, when they were beyond earshot of the road.

The giant began working at one hand as he walked. The hideous-looking knobs and scars peeled off. He applied a fluid from a small flask which he brought from a pocket, and the pallid texture of his skin turned into a grayish stain which he wiped off with a handkerchief. The hand, finally denuded of its disguise, was powerful and corded with tendons of startling size. In color, the hand was an unusual bronze hue, and the skin had a remarkably fine texture.

"The thing which started the shooting was very mysterious," the big man said slowly.

"Whatcha mean?" Monk queried.

The giant told briefly of the note, of the weird attack on Telegraph, of the shooting, of the disappearance of the note. His voice had changed from the rasping tone of the pugilist whom he had been portraying. It now possessed remarkable quality and a vibrant, restrained power.

"Blazes!" Monk exploded, when he had heard the recital. "That was a spooky business! Didn't their conversation explain it?"

"They discussed a man named Easeman and were very concerned over whether or not he was dead," said the big man. "They also did some conversing by a system of signaling on their hands. It must have been a system of their own, a sort of shorthand by gestures. There was not a movement for each letter of the alphabet, but motions which evidently meant whole phrases or sentences. Unfortunately, I failed to make out much of it."

He had rid his other hand of its disguise, and now went to work on his features. The malformities on his ears proved to be moulded of a rubberlike substance. Tiny metal forms spread its nostrils. Wax, removed from his cheeks, changed the whole contour of his features.

"What do you make of this whole thing, Doc?" Monk queried.

The giant was slow in replying.

"It is impossible to say," he stated finally. "I simply received that telegram from Boston, requesting me to be aboard the plane in disguise. The telegram was signed with a trick name meaning nothing."

He applied substance from the flask to his pale features, then wiped it off, and the transformation was little short of incredible. His countenance became one of remarkable handsomeness. The skin was the same amazing bronze hue as his hands. His hair, rid of its dye by the liquid in the flask, was of a bronze hue only slightly darker than his skin.

Plane noise marked the position of the airport ahead. The bronze giant veered off to the right, and shortly they came to his roadster, almost concealed in the clump of small trees into which he had driven it while trailing the fat Telegraph and the two fliers.

Monk demanded, "But Doc, what kind of a clue have we got to go on?"

"Telegraph told his driver to take them to the home of a man named Easeman, who has a daughter," Doc Savage explained.

Ham ejaculated, "But how did you get close enough to overhear——"

He did not finish. He had remembered their coming upon Doc Savage in the act of using the telescope. The bronze giant was an accomplished lip reader, along with a myriad of other abilities.

P. TREVE EASEMAN'S apartment was situated in one of the magnificent structures facing Central Park West. There were other Easemans listed in the telephone directory which Doc Savage had consulted, but none resided on Central Park West.

Doc parked in a side street adjacent to the apartment monolith and with Monk and Ham advanced toward the elaborate marquee entrance where two doormen stood, caparisoned as elegantly as naval admirals.

"*Ps-s-t!*" Monk hissed unexpectedly. "Lookit! Pullin' into the curb!"

Doc Savage said quietly, "Stopping to change clothing must have delayed them."

A dark sedan, large and expensive-looking, the chauffeur in rich livery, was nosing at the curb, and the two bedizened doormen clicked off salutes and wrestled with the door handles. The file of men who got out looked very dignified, very respectable in their immaculate full dress, complete even to white gloves, silk hats and shiny black evening sticks.

Telegraph led the parade. Four others followed him, all members of his organization who had taken part in the airport affair.

A boy, a lad who was noisy and none too tidy, ran up to the party alighting from the sedan. He waved newspapers.

"City's leading jeweler goes insane!" he bawled. "*Wux-t-r-a!* Read about it!"

One of the doormen said, "You cannot sell papers here."

"Jeweler sees jewels fly away and goes insane!" howled the urchin. "*Wux-t-ra p-o-iper!* Read about it!"

The doorman made an opening in one corner of his mouth and gritted, "Git outa here, you brat, 'fore I put a foot in your pants!"

Telegraph crinkled his round face with a pleasant smile, advanced, said, "A moment, please," and bought one of the urchin's newspapers. Then they entered the long, indirectly lighted lobby and confronted the prim-looking telephone operator.

"Mr. Edmunds and party to see Miss Ada Easeman," Telegraph announced.

The operator announced them over the house phone, then advised, "You are requested to go up."

Telegraph let his companions glance over the newspaper headlines as they were wafted upward on a silent elevator. The news story seemed to interest them greatly.

JEWELER UNBALANCED
TELLS WEIRD STORY

W. Carlton Smythe-Vancell, leading New York City jeweler, has been placed under the care of a psychiatrist, it was learned this evening.

Smythe-Vancell is reported to be suffering from the delusion that he saw a tray of his firm's most valuable jewels arise and float, unaided, from the showroom. The jewels, valued at only slightly less than a million dollars, are said actually to be missing. Police are on the case.

Telegraph and his men showed by not the slightest flicker that the item held interest for them, but when they had alighted in a tower corridor and the elevator had departed, one of the nattily clad group laughed dryly.

"A spook must have carried off those jewels," he chuckled.

"Very possible," Telegraph agreed. Then he eyed the fellow who had offered the remark about a spook. "What were the jewels actually worth?"

"A cool two million," said the other. "A fence has already bid a million, and he'll go even better."

Telegraph said calmly, "You gentlemen realize, of course, that this matter of the jewels was only what might be called a test of the efficiency of our discovery when directed along certain lines."

"*Certain lines* is right!" chuckled one of the men.

Telegraph stated with great satisfaction, "Gentlemen, we have the world at our feet!"

"It may take some convincing to make the world think so," offered another.

With a plump forefinger, Telegraph tapped the newspaper story about the jeweler who was supposedly demented.

"This is the first step," he advised. "As soon as we dispose of the matter of Easeman and Old Bonepicker, we shall have money to operate on a full scale."

The corridor down which they strode was one of tremendously rich furnishings. Coming to a door, they rang, and the panel was opened and they entered boldly. It was gloomy inside. They blinked more when blinding white light filled the room.

"Did you gentlemen ever see an automatic shotgun work

at close quarters?" a grimly determined feminine voice asked.

OBVIOUSLY, Telegraph and his neatly clad companions had control of their nerves, for they merely looked at the yawning snout of the shotgun, and with the exception of one who lost a cigarette hanging from his lip, none showed undue perturbation.

A young woman held the shotgun, and her manner of holding it was that of a trapshooter awaiting the rise of a clay bird. It was an action which showed she had handled a shotgun before.

"You will each seize the brim of your hat and yank it down over your eyes," she directed. "If you think I am bluffing merely don't take orders and see what happens!"

She had a throaty, educated voice which, holding no tremors, carried emphatic conviction.

"Quick!" she snapped. "Get those hats down over your eyes and blindfold yourselves!"

Her nails were enameled an unusual emerald hue. This tint exactly matched the low-backed, more than snug evening frock she wore.

Telegraph and his men pulled their hats down over their eyes. Then the girl ordered their hands up and moved among them, searching with deft fingers and removing guns from hip pockets and underarm holsters.

As the young woman moved about, it became evident that she was no ordinary bit of femininity. There was feline smoothness in her movements, along with the rippling play of more than ordinary muscular development in her arms and shoulders.

Telegraph spoke from under his hat, "My dear Miss Easeman, you are making a mistake. We are detectives——"

"——hired by my father as bodyguards before he disappeared," the girl took him up. "So you told me on a previous visit. And on that occasion you deftly pumped me to ascertain just what I knew about my father's disappearance. I suppose you came back this time for the same purpose?"

Telegraph began, "But my darling girl——"

"Rats!" said the young woman. "I found out who you are."

She herded them into a large, sumptuously furnished library and wrenched open the drawer of a massive table. From this she extracted two articles—a cocktail glass and a tiny camera which was composed largely of lens.

"I tried to seem very dumb on your previous visit," she said. "That was so I could get a chance to use this camera, which will take snapshots by ordinary electric light. And I also maneuvered you into leaving finger prints on this cocktail glass. I took the pictures and the finger prints to the police rogues' gallery."

This information caused Telegraph to sigh loudly.

"I must be slipping," he said.

"You certainly haven't lived up to your reputation," the girl told him. "A search of the rogues' gallery showed you to be 'Telegraph' Edmunds, one of the smoothest swindlers and confidence men in the country."

"Preposterous!" Telegraph Edmunds sighed, half-heartedly.

"You got the nickname of 'Telegraph' because of the system of gestures which you use to communicate with members of your gang," added the young woman.

This seemed to remind Telegraph Edmunds of something which he had overlooked. He cleaned a finger nail on his right hand with the thumb nail of his left. He brushed an imaginary speck from his cuff. One of the other men pressed the thumb and forefinger of his left hand together.

"Stop it!" rapped the girl. "You're talking to each other with your system of sign telegraphy!"

"Preposterous!" Telegraph repeated, and shrugged. His hands did not become still. They made more small gestures, motions which, one not suspecting, might have mistaken for minor nervousness but which the girl was sharp enough to recognize as more of the signals.

Her shotgun went off with an ear-splitting report.

TELEGRAPH screeched, fell to the floor. He tied himself into a knot and groveled, and his groans were hideous.

"Get up!" the girl grated, and menaced every one with the shotgun. "I fired over his head!"

Telegraph continued to squirm and moan. His convulsions brought him face upward, so that his countenance was visible. His visage was now drenched with red fluid. He moaned and scarlet bubbles puffed and burst on his full lips.

The girl seemed stunned. She became slightly pale. Her shotgun wavered.

One of the immaculately dressed men slid a toe out, hooked it behind a modernistic floor stand and kicked the piece of furniture at the girl. She side-stepped.

One of the other men snatched off his silk topper and hurled it at the girl. The range was short; the hat slapped her face hard.

The next instant, they were upon her, wrestling for the shotgun, which they got almost immediately. Three of them devoted almost their entire effort to holding the young woman.

Telegraph got up from the floor, used a handkerchief on

his face, and picked up the broken parts of a fountain pen which had been filled with red ink. He pocketed the pen fragments.

"A swell gag," he chuckled. "She was too busy watching everybody to see me smear it on my face."

Then he went to the outer door, opened it and listened for a long time, after which he made a quick circuit of the richly fitted apartment. He placed a guard in the outer corridor.

"This place occupies the whole floor and is probably just about soundproof," he decided. "Apparently nobody is going to investigate that shot."

The girl demanded angrily, "What do you want here?"

"My dear, we want to know where your father, P. Treve Easeman, can be found," Telegraph imparted calmly.

"I don't know where he is," the girl snapped.

Telegraph smiled without enthusiasm.

"You know, of course, what has happened to your father?" he stated.

"I do not," said the young woman. "Suppose you tell me."

Telegraph chuckled harshly. "That would be a bright move on my part."

Ada Easeman threw back her head.

"My father disappeared," she said grimly. "Since then, some strange things have happened. A large sum in cash disappeared from a safe here in the apartment, a safe to which only my father and myself had the combination. My father's broker has advised me that father telephoned him to sell certain bonds and stocks for cash. The broker did so, bringing the money to his office. The money disappeared mysteriously."

"It would seem that your father has been raising cash," said Telegraph.

"Yes," the girl retorted, "and you probably know why!"

"How much cash has he raised?" queried Telegraph.

"A great deal," Ada Easeman said coldly. "Somewhat over a million dollars."

Telegraph had been smiling, but it had not been a genuine smile. The smile now became hearty, actually joyful.

"This makes it look as if old Easeman actually intended to comply with our demands," he told his companions.

"But he was trying to fight us," one of them pointed out.

"Naturally," chuckled Telegraph. "But he got the money ready, which shows he intended to pay off if he had to."

The other grunted. "The thing to do is to whip Easeman in line somehow—if he's still alive."

"Still alive!" the girl cried out shrilly. "What do you mean?"

Telegraph produced a handkerchief and calmly jammed it between her jaws, doing it with the heel of his hand so that she would not bite him during the process.

"I know how we can stop Easeman," he said. "We'll give this girl the same thing we gave him."

"That should do it," the other agreed. "I hope you can straighten out the rest of it just as easy.

"What rest of it?" Telegraph demanded.

"The Doc Savage angle," the man explained.

Telegraph swore.

"We'll talk that over with the big boss," he growled. "He's a match for even this Doc Savage."

A deep, youthful voice said calmly, "I do believe this is what one would call a tableau!"

TELEGRAPH EDMUNDS was holding his silk topper with both hands. He dropped it, spun and faced the door which led to the outer corridor. His mouth became round with surprise.

"Careful!" he gulped at his men.

"Fitting advice, I call that," stated the deep, young voice.

The speaker stood squarely in the door. He was a lean man of more than average height and muscular build. Extremely black curly hair made him look even younger than he was; his pleasant features were tanned, and he had a waxed mustache which, in contrast with the darkness of his hair, was almost white. He looked efficient, worldly.

Clasped closely to his chest with a left arm, he held the lookout who had been posted in the outer corridor. The latter was unconscious. In his right hand, the young man with black hair and white mustache held a revolver, a large calibre gun built into a small frame. The weapon gave the impression of being composed mostly of barrel and cylinder.

"Have them yank their hats over their eyes so they can't see, Russ," the girl said, getting the gag out of her mouth. "That's the way I did."

"Excellent idea, I call that," smiled the young man.

Telegraph Edmunds made gritting noises with his teeth.

"Who is this bird?" he demanded.

One of Telegraph's gang answered the angry question.

"His name is Russel Wray," he said.

"I don't give a hoot what his name is," Telegraph growled. "Who is he? What is he?"

"He was Sawyer Linnett Bonefelt's bodyguard," advised the other.

"I have never heard of Sawyer Linnett Bonefelt," said Telegraph, pompous firmness in his manner.

"A gorgeous lie, I must say," snapped white-mustached, black-haired Russel Wray. "Sawyer Linnett Bonefelt has dropped out of sight just as P. Treve Easeman did. And you birds know something about it!"

Telegraph said smugly, "We are detectives hired by Easeman as bodyguards, just as you yourself were hired by Bonefelt. Our purpose seems to be the same. We should work together."

"I'll work a few chunks of lead into your systems!" Russel Wray threatened.

"Watch them, Russ!" the girl gasped. "They're lying! They are responsible for the disappearance of father and Old Bonepicker."

"Old Bonepicker?" Telegraph looked puzzled.

"That's what they call Sawyer Linnett Bonefelt, and don't tell me you didn't know it!" the girl snapped.

Telegraph started to say something in reply, but held the words back, and his jaw sagged, his plump hands made a vague gesture as if fending something off. He was watching the door.

The door led to the corridor, and its knob was turning slowly. The lock made a faint *click* as the bolt cleared the recess in the jamb. Then the panel opened slowly.

A horrible expression overspread Telegraph Edmund's visage.

"Watch out!" he screamed. "Watch out!"

Chapter 6

PHANTOMS

THE apartment structure had a height of nearly forty stories, and the P. Treve Easeman ménage was near the top, in the tower section, which was a smooth, chimney-like spile of masonry only a little less smooth than glass. The apartment house was not constructed of commonplace brick but of a polished gray native stone, and the blocks were set together without noticeable cracks.

To eavesdrop at the Easeman apartment windows, a man would have to scale the wall—and that was patently impossible. But there was a listener-in.

The eavesdropper was not a human listener-in, but an especially bulky contrivance of metal and wires and insulating composition. This was held to the window pane of the large library window by a rubber suction cup of the variety used to fasten ashtrays and other accessories to automobile windshields. The faint *thud* as this had been swung across the pane some time before, had escaped notice.

From the device, which an electrician woud have recognized as a highly sensitive microphone, wires led upward, passed over the roof coping and entered a box containing powerful audio amplifying apparatus. The sounds picked up by the window microphone finally entered a set of three ordinary headphones.

Doc Savage wore one headset. Monk and Ham wore the other two. They were very silent, listening raptly to what went on in the P. Treve Easeman library. They had eavesdropped on practically all that had been said from the first. The highly sensitive microphone had missed very little. They could hear Telegraph Edmunds shouting.

"Watch out!" he was screaming. "Be careful!"

Monk, the apish chemist, pulled one headphone away from an ear as if to hear himself talk and gulped, amazement in his small voice, "I'm a whatcha-call-it if I understand this!"

Strange sounds came over the listening device. Certain thumps were undoubtedly chairs upsetting; men groaned and grunted, and feet tapped parqueted flooring frantically. A vase or some other brittle bric-a-brac broke with a jangle which edged teeth. A man shrieked. The shriek was wordless, but it conveyed by its quality an awful horror and a mad fear.

"Sounds like a regular jamboree," Monk grunted.

"If you don't want a rib kicked in, shut up!" Ham told him shortly.

Doc Savage said nothing. It was a characteristic of the bronze man that he indulged in long periods of silence, rarely speaking, and never bandying idle conversation unless there was a purpose, some end to be gained.

Down in the Easeman apartment, a man wailed, "We can't whip the thing! It'll kill us all!"

"Don't call it a *thing!*" Telegraph Edmunds snarled. "You know what it is!"

There was more bedlam. Some one fired a gun. A splintery crash as a chair shattered indicated some one had swung with the piece of furniture.

"We haven't got a chance!" Telegraph Edmunds yelled suddenly, "Out of the apartment, everybody!"

A man barked, "What about the girl and this Russel Wray chick?"

"Let 'em stay here!" Telegraph rapped. "We gotta get to the big boss and talk things over! C'mon! Clear out!"

Sounds indicated the men were fighting their way toward the door.

Doc Savage hauled the headset from his ears.

"We're going down!" he said, and there was no trace of excitement in his remarkable voice.

Monk and Ham promptly charged for the hatch by which they had gained access to the roof, Monk pausing only long enough to grab up his pig, Habeas Corpus, by one oversize ear. Habeas seemed accustomed to this method of transportation.

Doc Savage tarried briefly. Beside the box containing the listening-in-device amplifier stood a second case of apparatus. He connected the two devices with a pair of flexible wires.

SINCE the P. Treve Easeman apartment was not far below the roof, they used the stairs rather than await arrival of an elevator.

Monk rumbled as he bounded down steps. Monk always became noisy when excited. His usually childlike voice became a bull bellow, and he had been known to stand in the middle of a fight, absolutely unhurt, and yell bloody murder merely for the sake of the noise.

"Swell stuff!" Monk rumbled. "We snoop around and listen in on the merry-go-round down in that apartment, and what does it get us? A headache!"

"Will you shut up?" Ham requested.

Monk continued. "We gumshoe around and we ain't got no more idea of what this is all about than when we started! Now if that ain't——"

They reached the corridor of the Easeman floor. The Easeman door was open. An airy rushing noise was coming from one of the elevator shafts. Otherwise, the hallway was extremely quiet.

Doc Savage whipped to the door and lunged inside. The rug was bunched, and scarlet smeared the floor. He went on. The library was a mess—furniture broken, askew, upset.

"Miss Easeman!" Doc called.

Silence answered.

"Wray!" The bronze man's voice was a crash.

There was more silence. Then a great smashing of glassware came from the kitchen regions. Doc whipped for the noise, came through a door and saw Ada Easeman and Russel Wray standing in a glittering lake of broken glass. They had evidently tried to move a cabinet to barricade the door and it had spilled its contents.

The girl did not look as if she had been through anything more strenuous than a débutante dance. Her emerald frock was unruffled, her hair undisturbed.

Contrasting with her immaculateness, Russel Wray's black hair was oozing red in two places, and a fist had mashed one spike of his waxed mustache into his lip, although the other spike stuck out straight and alert.

"What was the attacker?" Doc Savage asked.

Both stared. Neither spoke.

"What attacker?" Doc repeated, and there was in his unusual voice a quality which rapped out a demand for obedience.

Russel Wray spat noisily to get the mashed spike of his moustache away from his bruised lip. Then he spoke.

"I think they were crazy!" he said.

"What do you mean?" Doc demanded.

"There wasn't anybody!" Wray's voice was unclear because of his damaged lip. "The door opened. Then the gang began to jump around and yell and throw furniture. It was positively crazy!"

"Wait here, you two!" Doc Savage directed.

The bronze giant spun, crossed rooms, came out in the corridor and found Monk and Ham jabbing elevator buttons insistently. A moment later, a cage sighed to a stop and the doors whispered open. The three men dived inside with a suddenness which caused the operator to emit a frightened squawk.

Doc Savage himself dropped the cage toward the street level. There was excitement in the lobby. The telephone girl was a pale, motionless heap in her armchair, where she had fainted; the doorman was sitting down, crimson leaking through the fingers of both hands, which he kept pressed tightly over his face.

Monk, still carrying the pig by one huge ear, dashed out onto the street. He looked up and down the street. He put the pig down on the sidewalk.

"They got away," he said.

Doc and his men did not give up the pursuit immediately, although they would have profited as much to have done so, for there proved to be no substantial trail. Telegraph Edmunds and his men were a canny crew. They had not been picked up in flight by the same rich car in which they had arrived, but by another and much more shabby machine which had been parked near by, attracting no attention.

"Those birds are old heads," Monk offered.

Ham flourished his sword cane irately.

"The talk we overheard in that apartment didn't make sense," he snapped. "P. Treve Easeman and another man called Old Bonepicker have disappeared. The Easeman girl and Wray are scrapping with Telegraph Edmunds and his gang. Each accuses the other of knowing more than they told."

Monk picked up Habeas Corpus and scratched the bristles atop the homely shote's head, as if to encourage a thought process.

"What gets me," he said, "is that fight in the apartment. It sounded to me as if there was quite a scrap. But that bird Wray claimed there wasn't any attacker."

Both Monk and Ham eyed Doc Savage.

"What do you make of it, Doc?" Monk asked.

Instead of replying directly, the bronze man said, "We will talk the affair over with Ada Easeman and Russel Wray."

They entered the apartment house again.

An elevator operator, gape-mouthed with unsatisfied curiosity, let them out on the Easeman floor. They could hear the other elevators sighing in their shafts as they walked to the Easeman apartment. The door was closed. Doc tried it.

"Locked," Monk hazarded aloud when the panel did not yield.

The bronze man rapped. There was no response.

"Jove," Ham murmured. "They were supposed to wait here."

Monk squinted at the lock. "This baby is one of them new unpickable kind." He straightened. "We'd better try to get a key from the super."

Doc Savage moved a hand, not speaking, but the gesture indicating that the others should wait; then he took from his clothing a tiny case which held an assortment of probes and picks, and with these he went to work on the lock. Seemingly, he was unhurried, but hardly more than a minute elapsed before the elaborate tumblers surrendered and the door came open.

They entered and moved through rooms, stepping erratically and carefully that they might miss the crimson puddles on the floor, and from time to time calling out in a low voice. Not until they had gone through the entire apartment were they sure of the truth.

"The girl and Wray cleared out," Monk growled. "Now, what was the idea of that?"

"This don't look so good for Wray and the girl." Ham spun his sword cane in a manner a juggler would have envied. "They skipped, which bally well makes it seem they were afraid to talk to us."

Monk snorted loudly. "Then that yarn about nothing attacking Telegraph Edmunds and his gang and scaring them away was probably a fake."

Ham started a nod, then thought of something and almost dropped his spinning sword cane.

"A thought just came to me," he said.

"Be kind to it," Monk snorted. "It's in a strange place."

"Remember back in the woods by that road, after we followed Telegraph and his gang from the airport?" Ham demanded. "Telegraph and his men acted strangely there, acted as if something had attacked them—something that couldn't be seen."

"Something invisible?" Monk demanded.

"Quite right," Ham said.

"Nuts!" Monk told him.

Doc Savage said, "I suggest we go back to the roof for a few moments."

Monk and Ham registered puzzlement as they followed the bronze man up the stairway and out through the roof hatch. They had been associated with him long enough to know that he did not make idle suggestions, and they were puzzled to know what the roof could offer them in the line of assistance.

Catching sight of the listening-in-device, they seemed crestfallen, thinking the bronze man had merely come up to get the apparatus.

Doc Savage bent over the two cases of mechanism and began doing things with his sinewy fingers.

"Hey!" Monk ejaculated. "What's that other jigger?"

Instead of answering, Doc Savage opened the lid that the homely chemist might see the clockwork motor, the gears, the cylindrical black wax record and the voice-recording box which the case held.

"Voice recorder!" Monk grunted. "You hooked it on the listening device?"

That hardly called for an answer, for the bronze man tilted the recording box so that a play-back needle was brought in contact with the record, then changed connections of the headsets so that the voice line was picked up, amplified, then hurled into the receivers with remarkable intensity and fidelity of tone.

They heard sounds—mad sounds they were—of men running wildly, and realized these were the noises made by Telegraph Edmunds and his men in flight. Then there was an interval of silence, followed by the sound of Doc Savage's unusual voice calling out, "Miss Easeman!" "Wray!" Then there was the footstep noise of the bronze man entering.

So extremely sensitive was the pick-up that most of

what Doc Savage and the girl and Wray said back in the kitchen regions was not only audible, but understandable. The record had caught the noise of Doc's departure from the apartment.

Silence followed. Then came a surprise. Footstep noises indicated Wray and the girl had come back into the library.

"Who was that big bronze man?" asked a voice.

The speaker was not Wray. It was a male voice, however, but one which neither Doc Savage nor his men had heard previously. There was a strained, unnatural quality about the voice, a tang of unreality, and it was very coarse, an aged voice, querulous.

Response to the words was startling. The girl shrieked softly. Wray barked something surprised and unintelligible.

"Who was he?" the strange voice repeated.

"Old Bonepicker!" the girl cried out in a shrill, amazed voice. "What are you doing here?"

"I followed that devil Telegraph Edmunds," said the voice. "I've been following him ever since he arrived in a plane this afternoon. I've been hoping he would lead me to his boss, the master mind who is behind what he is doing. Now, who was that bronze man?"

"Doc Savage," said the girl.

"Hm-m-m," mumbled the strange voice. "Who brought him in?"

"My father," said the girl. "Telegraph Edmunds had been holding my father in Boston to keep him from getting in touch with you. They did not know that you had already started working together, through myself and Russel Wray, here. Father telegraphed Doc Savage to be on the Boston plane today."

"Bad," said the voice which the girl had attributed to the mysterious "Old Bonepicker." "Your father should not have brought Doc Savage into this. It will only excite these devils. They will start operations on a large scale. Left alone, your father and myself might have accomplished something. If they get stirred up and really cut loose, we'll be helpless. The world will be in a terrible shape, because all of the policemen and all of the armies and navies won't be able to help a bit!"

"I was afraid of the same thing," said the girl.

"Something has happened to your father," said the querulous voice.

The girl made a loud gasping sound of horror.

"Now don't get hysterical," snapped Old Bonepicker. "You go out to the airport and see what you can find. You do that, see?"

"We will," the girl agreed.

Chapter 7

THE SPOOK AT THE AIRPORT

THAT was the end of the recorded sounds, and Doc Savage clicked off the switches and hurriedly packed the apparatus for transportation. Monk helped. Ham, who was no great mechanic, stood by and vouchsafed remarks.

"So the trail leads back to that airport!" he snorted. "I wonder just what we missed out there!"

Monk glanced at a window.

"Gonna be dark before we get out there," he offered.

Ham tilted his sword cane. "Are we going to the jolly airport?"

Doc Savage said, "It is the best lead."

Down on the street, they found traffic thick enough to hamper progress, but there was a police siren under the hood of Doc Savage's car, and the license plates bore distinct numerals of very low denomination, a combination which enabled them to split traffic wide open in the dash over the long elevated roadway to the airport at which the excitement had occurred earlier in the afternoon.

Doc cut the headlights when they pulled off the main highway and drove by the glow of the moon. He parked before getting near enough that the car might be heard, and they went on afoot.

Monk, carrying Habeas by an ear, lifted on tiptoe to eye the black, silent humps of the hangars, the regular and brilliant white splash of the beacon, and the array of colored lights marking the tarmac confines.

"Plumb peaceful," he offered.

They did not approach the hangars by way of the main entrance, but surmounted the high metal guard fence some two hundred yards distant and went forward, crouching in the concealment of an ornamental hedge which paralleled the metal fence. It was with scarcely a sound that they eased into the big hangar which held the transport plane that had arrived that afternoon from Boston.

Monk breathed. "We look for a guy named P. Treve Easeman—is that it?"

Doc Savage was silent a moment.

"You go over the plane interior, Monk," he directed. "Ham and I will examine the hangar itself."

Monk grunted, "But them birds this afternoon searched the plane."

Doc Savage said nothing, and Monk, shrugging, got the cabin door open and, still carrying his pig by an ear, swung inside. He put the shote down.

"Go get 'em, Habeas," he directed.

THE pig stood perfectly still. He sniffed. Bristles on his neck and back hackled up, dog-fashion.

Monk, busy examining the cabin by the aid of a tiny flashlight which had a spring generator instead of a battery, missed the significance of the shote's actions. Monk started with the pilot compartment and worked aft, examining each seat as he came to it. He roved his flash beam over the cushions.

Well aft, he came to a seat, the cushion of which was stained in a rather queer fashion. Monk scrutinized the stain closely. It puzzled him. He reached down and touched it.

He nearly jumped out of his skin and dropped the flashlight, which rolled under the seat. The cushion *felt* wet.

Monk hurriedly got down on all fours, retrieved the light, twisted the lens head so that the beam was wider, then turned the illumination on the seat. He touched the stain again, felt a distinctly wet sensation and eyed his fingers, expecting to see something. There was nothing.

The fingers still felt wet, and he hastily wiped them on his trouser leg. An instant later, it felt as if a wet liquid, wiped from his fingers, had soaked through the trouser fabric to the bare skin.

Monk winked small eyes. The light went out and he re-wound the spring generator with wild haste. Then he reached around to smooth down certain hairs on the back of his neck, hairs which felt as if they were standing on end.

He hesitated, then touched the cushion and transferred his finger tips to his lips. He spat violently. There had been a distinctly salty taste.

Forward in the cabin the pig, Habeas Corpus, squealed shrilly.

Monk heaved up on his feet. The pig was back against a seat, tusks bared. The animal looked scared. Monk lunged down the aisle.

Two steps, and he emitted a howl that could not have been louder had he been unexpectedly stabbed.

Doc Savage and Ham were scrutinizing the far end of the hangar, devoting more of their time in listening than in searching, in hopes of hearing either Wray or the girl. When Monk yelled, both spun sharply.

"Monk!" Doc rapped. "What is it?"

"Blazes!" Monk bawled. "There's somethin' screwy about this crate!"

They could see the homely chemist through the plane windows. He was crouched like a great ape, moving forward cautiously, the flashlight beam roving. Suddenly, Monk paused. He stared. His small eyes seemed to swell in their sockets.

One of the seat cushions in front of him was distinctly sinking. It was if a weight were bearing down on it. But there was nothing to be seen!

Monk held his breath. The pig was tense. Forward in the cockpit, a pair of clocks ticked in mechanical concert.

Then—and Monk afterward swore that it stood his hair permanently on end—there was a groan. It was a very distinct and awful groan. The sound had such a hoarse quality that it was difficult to tell from where it came.

Monk moved. He had to do something, if only jump. He drifted a hand out to grasp a chair and help himself in the direction of the door. He never took hold of the chair. Instead, his fingers encountered something faintly warm—and *wet*.

Monk fell back into his habit of yelling when he was excited.

"*Whew!*" he howled. "Blazes! For the love of mud!"

At the other end of the hangar, Ham yelled, "Stop that noise, you missing link!"

"Spooks!" Monk bawled. "There's a danged spook in this sky chariot!"

Doc Savage and Ham both ran toward the plane.

They did not reach the ship. One of the huge sliding hangar doors came back with a whirring of track rollers. Men popped through. They wielded powerful hand searchlights and an assortment of submachine guns and ordinary pistols.

Telegraph Edmunds led the rush.

The homely Monk, in the plane, forgot his spook troubles. He snapped a red-bristled hand to his armpit and brought out one of the compact super-machine pistols which resembled overgrown automatics.

The plane windows were of non-shatter glass. He banged one out with a fist, leveled the machine pistol and tightened down on the trigger. A whooping moan filled the great hangar.

The gun was charged with mercy bullets, a type which did not kill but produced unconsciousness in the course of such a few seconds that it seemed their effects were instantaneous.

When Telegraph Edmunds did not go down immediately, Monk was not surprised. But when the plump Telegraph spun, dived for a pile of oil drums and reached them without incident, Monk was somewhat astonished. He was even more surprised when Telegraph began to shoot deliberately at him with an automatic pistol.

Then the explanation dawned on Monk.

"Them guys have got bulletproof vests!" he howled.

Then he ducked. The transport plane was no armored war craft. Revolver bullets cut through it with invisible viciousness. Monk dived for the door, reached it, tumbled out and ran toward Doc Savage and Ham.

Ham had tucked his sword cane under an arm and unlimbered another of the supermachine pistols. He fired, and the slugs splashed their chemical content on the oil drums behind which the assailants had taken cover. A foe cursed and his profanity smothered off in a way which showed he had been hit effectively by one of the mercy slugs.

Telegraph Edmunds was grumbling orders, and in a moment his men began placing their flashlights on top of the drum, so that the blinding beams ranged the hangar, illuminating Doc Savage and his two companions.

Monk slapped prone on the floor. Shooting together, he and Ham hurriedly wiped out the row of glittering flashlight eyes. It was nice marksmanship.

Telegraph swore distinctly and feelingly.

"Get to the damned plane!" he howled. "We want that spook the ape of a guy was yelling about!"

Monk, scuttling swiftly, reached Doc Savage and Ham about the time these words were shouted. The homely chemist grunted unbelievingly, and perhaps with some relief.

"There was sure somethin' strange in that plane," he muttered. "I tell you, I felt something salty and wet where there wasn't anything!"

"Hallucinations," said Ham.

"Who?" Monk demanded, not catching the word.

A bullet struck near by, scouring up concrete fragments, and Monk and Ham hastily inched backward. Their own lights were out now. It was dark in the hangar, the only illumination being starlight which spilled in through the open sliding door.

"Doc, what d'you reckon is in that plane?" Monk asked.

There was no answer.

"Doc," Monk repeated.

Then he felt about. There was no trace of the bronze man.

At the moment that Monk was putting his question, Doc Savage was working along the hangar wall some yards distant. He traveled with the silence of a phantom, but did not go far. He paused, observing that there was light enough ahead—the glow of moonbeams which came through the door —to disclose his figure.

The hangar was of rugged construction, sheet metal over large steel beams, and the bronze man grasped one of the latter and began to ascend. It was no miraculous climb, but it was tedious, for only the tight clamp of his fingers on the vertical fins of the beams kept him up.

A man with an ordinary set of muscles would have mounted ten feet, possibly fifteen if he were in good trim. It was some forty feet to the top, and after that, there was a labyrinth of beams to traverse in intense blackness, with a misstep meaning a death drop to the hard concrete floor far below.

The door tracks were high up, and by crouching to one side Doc Savage managed to put sudden weight against the panels and send them whirring shut. The darkness which clamped down inside the hangar was intensely black.

Telegraph swore. So did some of his men. They shot at the door, raking the panel, thinking some one had reached it from the floor level.

Monk and Ham opened up with their superfirers.

Telegraph cursed some more. The supermachine pistols had special compensators built into the muzzles which, in addition to balancing recoil, digested muzzle flame so that it was difficult to spot the little weapons.

Doc Savage changed his position, having slow going in spite of his tremendous muscular strength, and reached another vertical girder. He went down this, using only the grip of cabled hands, and touched the floor directly behind the oil drums which sheltered Telegraph and his gang.

It is virtually impossible for a man to move in the darkness without making at least some sound. The men behind the oil drum barricade might have heard the bronze giant descending had not they been concentrating on the fight. As it was, the sounds they were making guided Doc in his attack.

The first victim made a stifled mewing sound that might have come from a very hungry cat. That much of a noise squeezed past the tremendous clutch of bronze fingers which fell upon his throat.

Doc did not try to exert throttling pressure. Instead, he used upon the man a device which he had discovered in the course of anatomical research upon the human brain, and which he had mastered by long practice. He felt about, located certain nerve centers with his finger tips, and bore down with a sharp, paralyzing pressure which rendered the victim unable to move or speak for some time.

One of the others heard the noise. He lunged, feeling with his hands, and his clutching fingers encountered Doc Savage. The next instant the fellow was reeling backward from a tremendous blow in the face. He emitted a howl.

Across the hangar, Monk and Ham heard the shout, guessed what had caused it and began to yell and fire their machine pistols. The combination of noise and danger was too much for the hangar attackers.

"This is too tough!" Telegraph grated. "Clear out!"

They surged up in a wild charge for the door. The sliding panel had secured itself in some fashion. It resisted. Three of them got one behind the other and hurled their combined weights against a sheet of the metal hangar covering. The sheet split and let them out into the night.

THE earlier quietness about the airport did not mean that it was deserted, but only that the personnel were having a slack hour, and were gathered, talking, in the operations office. The shooting, the yelling, had stirred up a turmoil. The landing lights, tremendous flood lenses spraying incandescence that was almost hot daylight, had been switched on. Some of the men were armed. Pilots carrying mail were authorized to have firearms.

Members of the airport personnel yelled questions. Telegraph swore and drove a flurry of bullets over their heads.

Instead of fleeing, the airport force scattered, cutting off flight in the direction of the road. They began shooting. One of Telegraph's men bellowed and fell, clawing at the hole which a bullet had opened in his leg.

Telegraph glared at his party. They were not a mobile force, since they were carrying those who had been overcome by the mercy bullets in the hangar, as well as the pair made unconscious by Doc Savage.

Angrily, Telegraph jabbed a pudgy hand at the senseless burdens.

"Can't leave 'em!" he groaned. "This Doc Savage will grab 'em and make 'em talk!"

"We can fix it so they can't talk," some one reminded.

"Don't be a nut!" Telegraph grunted. "Good men are too scarce."

One of the men yelled, sloped an arm.

"Why not use that buggy?" he barked.

The "buggy" was a single-motored cabin monoplane—a new ship if its bright paint and shiny metal were any indications. There was a neat canvas jacket over the motor.

The men ran toward the plane. One gave a leap, seized the canvas cover and yanked it off, then ran around and yanked at the door. It was locked. He beat in a window with a pistol and got to the door and unlatched it from the inside.

Telegraph Edmunds was hanging back, showing little enthusiasm for the plane escape.

"They'll take off in another ship and follow us!" he barked.

"Sure!" snapped one of the others. "But we can't get to our car carrying these birds."

"The plane won't hold all of us," Telegraph shouted angrily. "Some of you take the unconscious men and get in the air. The rest of us will make a try for the cars."

They proceeded to carry this suggestion out. Telegraph and three companions keeping a steady fire directed at such men as exposed themselves around the airport. The plane motor was equipped with a starter; this turned the motor smashing over noisily. The pilot—one of the gang was a flier—gave the cylinders little time to warm but opened the throttle, and the plane kicked its tail up and scudded across the tarmac.

Telegraph and the others ran for the edge of the field, dropping flat at intervals to shoot the floodlights out, so that they were enveloped in darkness.

It became evident that they were going to make good their escape.

Doc Savage, Monk and Ham were doing about all they could do—striving to head off the escape. They were handicapped. Telegraph and his men seemed to have plenty of ammunition, and were not at all reluctant about expending it. Once, the airport attendants mistook them for enemies and turned loose a storm of lead, driving them to cover. They shouted angrily, trying to convince the skeptical attendants they were not foes. By the time they succeeded, the plane bearing Telegraph's men was in the air, and Telegraph Edmunds himself was near the field edge.

Doc Savage and his men set out after the group fleeing on the ground.

An attendant ran to a powerful searchlight and turned it upon the plane. The craft was circling, gaining altitude, and evidently standing by to offer aid, should necessity arise, to Telegraph himself. The ship was a glittering, buzzing monstrosity in the brilliant searchlight glitter.

Telegraph and his three companions scrambled wildly over the high metal fence bounding the airport. He paused, rested a gun on the fence wire and fired, but his other men, clambering over, shook the fence until the bullets went wild.

Doc Savage reached the fence a hundred yards distant. He did not run to it and climb, but attacked the barrier like a cat, with a tremendous leap which lifted him nearly to the top. He landed lightly on the other side. Then he stood there, attention suddenly fixed on the plane.

Something was happening to the craft. It dipped, wabbled. It seemed on the verge of cracking up. Then it straightened out and, motor a-howl, swooped upward. The searchlight followed it.

Monk and Ham now stared at the plane. Its antics were fantastic.

"Hey!" Monk exploded. "Somebody threw a parachute overboard!"

The small packet of the parachute was barely distinguishable in the intense searchlight glitter. It descended slowly, not turning over and over as it fell, as might have been expected. Then something unexpected occurred.

"Blazes!" Monk gulped. *"Look at that!"*

The parachute had opened, blossoming into a great mushroom of snowy silk. It did not fall as loose cloth might have. It held its belled shape. Below it, the shrouds stretched rigidly, as if supporting a weight. But there was nothing visible in the harness.

"Observe the plane!" Ham snapped.

The ship had resumed its antics. It nosed up too steeply, stalled, slid off in a spin, and did not recover. The motor mumbled at ordinary speed, but the flying wires began to howl in a fashion that could be heard a great distance.

The craft was probably traveling in excess of three hundred miles an hour when it hit the ground. The searchlight followed it to the last. Flying earth and debris geysered upward. Then there was a sheet of white flame, as if a photographer's flash gun had gone off. This lasted only momentarily, and left a bundling mass of redder flames which had enwrapped the whole craft.

Doc Savage shifted his attention to the parachute. It was coming down on the tarmac. The harness touched the field. The night breeze carried the big lobe over, and it dragged the harness along. The harness was not touching the ground, but elevated nearly two feet. And below the webbing straps there was a disturbance. Dust stirred up. Clods of earth were dislodged. Two shallow grooves appeared. They might have been made by a pair of heels.

Monk bawled, "Does anybody else see what I see?"

Ham still retained his sword cane. He fumbled it absently. "There is something on that 'chute!" he gulped. *"Something you can't see!"*

THE airport attendants, as stunned as any one, ran for the 'chute, some for the crashed plane.

Doc Savage said, "Telegraph Edmunds! We'll trail him!"

The bronze man and his two aides ran in pursuit of Telegraph. The latter, with his three companions, had paused to witness the disaster to the plane and the mysterious parachute descent, but now they began running. They were not far ahead, but were fast on their feet, for they were scared. Gaining the edge of the flying field, they turned sharply to the left, diving into a brushy lane. A moment later, the motor of a car they had concealed there began to moan.

The machine—a sedan—lumbered into view. Monk lifted his machine pistol and drove a hooting volley of slugs. They flattened on the sedan windows.

"Bulletproof!" Monk snorted.

The sedan windows, it developed, cranked aside enough to allow a slit which would admit a gun muzzle. Men began firing through these, using submachine guns. Doc Savage and his two aides, possessed of no quality which made them impervious to lead, sought the roadside ditch.

The sedan betook itself noisily away.

Doc Savage said, "Our own car!"

They ran back to where they had parked their machine, entered it and tramped the starter. Nothing happened. Doc wrenched up the hood, dashed a flash beam inside, then pointed.

The wiring had been torn out. Stepping back, the bronze man examined the soft earth around about, noting the size of the impressed tracks. Among other things, he had developed a facility for retaining accurate optical measurements in his memory; he could look at a print and recognize instantly, hours later, another print made by the same shoe. He had seen Telegraph Edmunds's footprints during the afternoon.

"These are Edmunds's tracks," he said quietly. "He disabled our car."

Over on the airport fence the pig, Habeas Corpus, was clambering up the high barrier, having some difficulty and squealing plaintively. Monk helped the shote over.

"We're getting nowhere fast," he complained. "Seems like things are breaking so we can't learn a thing."

"We know one thing!" Ham snapped. "There are invisible things of some kind mixed up in this."

The homely Monk scowled at the dapper barrister.

"I always did know you'd study law until you went nuts," he said.

Ham gritted, "Then how do you explain that parachute business? And didn't you feel something in the plane cabin?"

Monk dangled Habeas by an ear, and said nothing. His apish features wore a baffled expression.

They went back to the airport grounds to examine the wrecked plane. There was a crowd. Two fire extinguisher wagons had been run out and were playing chemical streams on the wrecked plane. But they were too late. Flames had consumed most of the ship.

It was doubtful if any of the bodies inside could be identified.

Doc Savage ferreted out the airport attendants who had been first to reach the mysterious parachute and questioned them, extracting information which did nothing to explain what had occurred, for the attendants insisted there had been no one near the 'chute.

Asked to explain the manner in which it had come down, they were vague, and finally tried to laugh it off as a freak occurrence.

"It was screwy, though," one of them admitted. "After the 'chute collapsed, the webbing harness jumped around as if something were getting out of it. Then it fell to the ground."

Doc Savage said, "Let us examine the spot where the 'chute came down. There may be marks on the ground."

They might as well have saved their time. Excited persons going and coming from the burning plane, had stamped out whatever tracks there might have been.

Police arrived, and made the mistake of devoting all of their energy to clearing the crowd from about the plane, extinguishing the flames and extracting the charred bodies. It was some minutes before they got organized on the matter of the shooting.

Doc Savage got his two aides aside.

"We can answer police questions later," he said. "We will leave now."

That decision was a mistake, one of the few in judgment errors which the bronze man had made. But, remarkable as was his trained mind, it had no powers of clairvoyance, and he could not see into the future.

There was one more unexpected happening. It occurred as they left the airport.

"Over there!" the bronze man said suddenly, and pointed. His two assistants, following his indicating arm, saw the figures of a man and a woman. They were walking close together, staggering a little. Their arms were out, but not around each other. Rather, the arms seemed to support something between them, something which, as far as visual evidence went, was not there.

The two forms came in range of automobile headlights. Their identity was apparent.

"The girl, Ada Easeman, and that guy, Russel Wray!" Monk roared. He hurtled toward the pair.

Ada Easeman and Russel Wray reached a car, an open touring which had the top down. They seemed to have some difficulty getting in, and it seemed that they were helping their unseen burden. The girl got behind the wheel, and the machine, tires spouting gravel, rocketed away long before Doc Savage, for all his sprinting speed, was near enough to stop them.

"Seize a car!" Doc rapped.

The nearest machine was a taxicab, which had evidently brought a passenger out to the airport. The driver had just gotten out and was running toward the burning plane. All of his interest was on the flaming ship. He did not look back as Doc Savage, Monk and Ham entered the cab, started the motor and drove in pursuit of the girl and Wray.

The hack was neither new nor in good mechanical shape; when weight was put on the accelerator, a carbon knock tinkled and a piston slap made angrier accompaniment. The speedometer needle bogged before it reached fifty.

The touring car bearing the girl and Wray was probably doing eighty when it went out of sight.

DOC SAVAGE slowed down and the cab seemed to run even more noisily, while an overheated smell came from the motor. The wheel had a distinct list to the right.

"There oughta be a law against a heap like this," Monk grumbled. "Boy, are we having tough luck!"

The engine stopped suddenly.

Doc Savage, at the wheel, remained as motionless as if graven in the bronze metal which he resembled, except for the slight shift of his arms as he coasted the car to the edge of the pavement and put on the brakes. The brakes squealed like pigs.

"Hurrah!" Monk snorted. "Now we can walk back."

Doc Savage's lips seemed scarcely to move as he spoke.

"Look at the switch," he suggested.

Monk squinted at the key. "Huh! It's off!" He moved to turn the key on.

"Wait!" Doc told him, and started to add something more,

but the pig, Habeas Corpus, emitted a series of uneasy grunts.

Monk frowned at the shote, which was in the rear seat, and demanded, "What ails you?"

Doc Savage's voice was emotionless as he spoke.

"I think there is something in the car with us," he said. "Something we cannot see. It turned the switch off!"

Monk gulped, "Well, for—" and could think of no adequate finishing phrase.

They all eyed the switch which had turned off so strangely. It was Doc Savage who saw the rear door opening. He whipped open the door on his side, dived out and flung for the other door.

The door slammed just before he reached it. He clutched madly at the air. Apparently he encountered nothing, for he stood still and seemed to listen. Then he leaped far to the left and clutched again.

"No use," he said. His voice showed neither disgust nor excitement.

The homely Monk demanded loudly, "Am I going nuts?"

Ham clenched his sword cane tightly.

"There was something in here," he said. "It got out, whatever it was, after it turned the switch off."

Doc Savage came back to the taxi, opened the rear door and got inside slowly, his hands groping, searching, but finding nothing. His eyes, however, located something of interest, for he leaned down and thumbed on a flashlight.

"Look here," he requested.

The cab rear was lined with rather ancient leather. Some sharp object—it was probably a screw which had come loose from the meter fastening and now lay on the floorboards—had scratched a number of words in the leather. They read:

Savage:
Go to opera to-night.

There was no signature.

Monk finished reading, drew back, absently started to scratch his own head, then scratched the bristles atop Habeas Corpus's nodular skull instead.

"They do say music uplifts the soul," he said. "Personally, I never felt less like going to the opera."

Doc Savage consulted a wrist watch which had a jeweled, shockproof movement.

"The performance is already on," he said. "But we can make the end of it."

Ham sheathed and unsheathed his sword cane.

"That invisible thing, whatever it was, must have been able to write," he said slowly.

Chapter 8

TERROR AMONG ERMINES

THE structure that is the center of operatic America, the citadel which draws the crowned heads of the profession for their finest performances, is a building which outwardly resembles an enormous and very grimy warehouse. Viewed from the street, it offers nothing impressive other than its size, except on opera nights, when it takes on a dignity and an aura of glittering impressiveness.

Doc Savage, Monk and Ham left the Times Square subway station and worked southward toward the opera house. The bronze man rarely wore a hat, but he had donned one now, yanked far down, and his coat collar was turned up. He did not wish to be recognized.

He was, against his own inclinations, a celebrity, thanks to the industry of newspaper reporters. Should he be recognized, a crowd of curious individuals and autograph hunters was sure to collect.

There was some delay at the opera house. None of the three wore full dress, and they looked somewhat disheveled. Nor did they have tickets; and the house was sold out. Or so the young man at the ticket window said.

Doc Savage made known his identity.

"I beg your pardon," bowed the young man at the window. "I did not recognize you. I will have an usher take you to your box."

Monk eyed Doc Savage as they were escorted inside.

"How long has this been going on?" he wanted to know.

"You mean the box? I have had that some time; in fact, my father had it before me."

Monk digested that, and wondered just how much the bronze man contributed for use of the box. Plenty, no doubt. Monk remembered that there had been talk of an unnamed contributor who had lifted the operatic enterprise from its financial dilemma. The bronze man had a habit of doing things like that.

"Hey!" Monk barked. "Whatcha think you're doin'?"

The usher had grasped Habeas Corpus by the scruff of the neck and was preparing to take him away.

"Animals not allowed," the usher explained.

Ham indicated Monk with his sword cane and suggested, "The ape falls in that class, too. Better take him."

Monk, bristling indignantly, declared, "That hog is a well-behaved hog, and he likes music. He stays here!"

There was more squabbling, but when the usher departed Habeas remained behind, perched on the rail in plain view of the audience, ears distended to catch the booming of a dark and extremely fat basso.

The performance had reached a point where the fat basso was whooping and moaning in the throes of indecision about whether to surrender an equally plump prima donna to the arms of the rival who sang tenor.

"I guess it'll be over when he makes up his mind," muttered Monk, who had no great appreciation of fine music. "That'll probably take another five minutes."

Over in the diamond horseshoe, a woman screamed suddenly and with a volume that made the high note of the prima donna on the stage seem small in comparison.

MONK said, "I knew that basso would drive somebody nuts!" Then he stood up and stared. He shed his wisecracking manner, howled, "Hey! Lookit!"

The woman who had shrieked was long and bony and much bejeweled. An ermine wrap was in disarray about her shoulders, and she was clutching madly with both hands. She shrieked again.

The article at which she grabbed was a diamond pendant, a diamond that was very large and caught subdued fire from the lights on the stage. It seemed suspended in mid-air, as if by an unseen string, before the woman's face. It moved as she snatched at it, causing her to miss.

Then a jeweled band about the woman's hair seemed to jump from its anchorage. The woman screamed as her hair was yanked. The gaudy band joined the pendant. The woman continued to shriek.

There was a smacking sound, loud enough that Doc Savage and his men heard it distinctly over the squawling of the woman, and she collapsed, as if knocked out.

"The invisible thing!" Monk rapped.

Doc Savage was already out of the box. An ornamental rail ran along the fronts of the boxes, joining them, and the bronze man sprang upon this, running along it. The main floor was more than a score of feet below, and a drop would have meant at least bad injury upon the seats.

Farther down the row of boxes, another woman began to

flounce about and shriek. She seemed to be losing large rings off her fingers. Almost instantly there was a third disturbance.

"The spooks are robbing these people!" Monk gulped.

He got up on the rail with the idea of following the bronze man, but took one look below and scrambled off again. He charged out of the box and through the aisles.

Ham unsheathed his sword cane and followed the apish chemist, making passes at apparently empty air with the blade.

"Careful!" he rapped at Monk. "You cannot see the infernal creatures."

Monk heard, wheeled back and scooped up his pet pig.

"Habeas seemed to be able to smell them, or something, before," he said; then to the pig, "Do your stuff, hog!"

Doc Savage had reached the tall, bony woman who had shrieked first. He drove bronze fingers about, searching, but encountered nothing. The jewels had seemed to drop down and had become lost in the gloom of the aisles. Best efforts of his flake-gold eyes failed to locate them.

There was a growing bruise on the woman's jaw, mark of the mysterious blow which had knocked her senseless.

The bronze man rushed for the next victim. There, too, he found nothing. Other women were howling as they lost their jewels. Ushers were rushing about. One tripped and fell down one of the sloping aisles, and opera patrons, leaving their seats madly, piled over him in a mêlée.

Doc Savage fanned a glance about and located a young woman who wore a particularly expensive-looking collection of jewels. He ran toward her. Before he reached her, she ripped out a cry of horror and struck at the air before her. One of the invisible beings seemed to have grabbed at her jewels, and she had avoided the grasp. She spun and fled, racing up the aisle toward a red light that marked an exit.

Doc followed, tremendous leaps closing the gap between himself and the fleeing woman. She dived into the dark cavern under the scarlet exit lamp. There the bronze man caught her.

"Stand still!" he commanded.

"Something touched me!" the woman gurgled. "Something which I could not see——"

There was a sudden ugly sound. It was a hollow report, very much as if a hammer had hit some hard substance.

Doc Savage fell as if all of his giant sinews had been severed simultaneously.

THE woman with the jewels fell from a second, far less

violent blow a moment later. Her baubles left her person and came together making clicking noises, as if they were being dropped in an absolutely transparent container.

The nap of the carpet beside Doc Savage crushed down as if an unseen weight were bearing upon it. One of his hands lifted, but in a strangely lifeless manner, and the bronze skin over one wrist acquired a depression that might have meant his pulse was being tested.

There was a short peculiar whistling sound, the kind of a whistle by which a man might summon a dog.

From the darker recess down the fire escape corridor a metal tray floated, an ordinary tray of the type used by housewives to bake muffins, divided off into ten cups. In each of these cups reposed reddish, soft-looking wax. The tray came to a rest on the floor beside Doc Savage's right hand.

One by one, the bronze man's fingers were lifted and pressed into the soft wax, making an impression in which the whorls and lines of the finger tips were distinct. The tray shifted to the other side, and the same thing happened to his left hand.

The tray floated away and was lost in the darkness.

The jewels had remained suspended in mid-air, but now they also swung away without visible suspension, the manner of their going something to lift the hair of a superstitious observer, had there been one.

Doc Savage remained, limp and unstirring, where he had been felled. His features had slammed the floor heavily when he went down, and small crimson bubbles broke at his lips from time to time, showing that he still breathed.

The opera house was in an uproar, with women shrieking and men bawling out in rage and fright, while down on the stage, the fat basso sang at the top of his voice, a lilting tune that was calculated to quiet the clamor, but which failed completely.

Police whistles shrilled as an emergency squad bored into the opera house.

Chapter 9

MARIKAN

MONK beat an open newspaper with one hairy fist and said, small-voiced, "Look at this! Look at it!"

Ham looked up wearily from his task of daubing a fresh supply of chemical, intended to produce quick unconsciousness, upon the tip of his sword cane.

"Will you stop ranting?" he requested. "This thing is crazy enough without you adding your nickel's worth."

It was cool in the gigantic laboratory with its labyrinth of chemical and electrical apparatus. The coolness was that of artificial air conditioning. The huge windows were closed; they always remained closed. They were of bullet-proof glass.

Through the windows, the tallest of New York's skyscrapers could be seen, for these windows were on the eighty-sixth floor of the city's most impressive cloud-piercer. Beyond the tips of the higher buildings, the city was a checkerboard of lights. It was an aerie of masterly situation, this headquarters of Doc Savage.

The bronze man himself was seated in the maze of an X-ray machine, employing mirrors and fluoroscopic screens in such a manner that he could examine his own head. He was kneading a spot over the temple.

"The blow seems to have been delivered with something resembling a blackjack," he offered quietly. "It did no great damage."

"Look at this paper!" Monk repeated. "It says that over four hundred policemen got down to that opera house before the excitement subsided. They had bomb squads, detective squads and homicide squads. They even had the fire department."

"We know all about that," Ham told him peevishly. "We were jolly well there, weren't we?"

"And the sum total of what all the cops found was just exactly nothing," Monk continued, ignoring Ham. "They won't even admit for publication that invisible beings had something to do with the affair."

Doc Savage put in, "It is rather a preposterous thing for a hard-headed policeman to believe."

Monk wrinkled his remarkably homely features in a scowl.

"Whatever the robbers were, they sure made a clean-up of jewelry," he imparted.

"Is an estimate of the amount given?" Doc asked.

"One paper says it will run as high as four or five millions," Monk advised. "Can't tell much by newspaper guesses, though."

Doc Savage did not comment further, but seemed engaged in making a complete examination of his own person. He came around to his finger tips and gave them a great deal of attention. He scraped a small deposit of reddish substance from under one of the nails, took it over to a spec-troscopic analyzing device and worked over it.

"What'd you find?" Monk queried.

"A material which I have no recollection of touching," the bronze man explained.

"What is it?"

"A form of modeling wax which is used when soft and later becomes very hard," Doc announced.

"Yeah?" Monk nudged the pig, Habeas, with a toe. "Where could you have picked the wax up?"

The bronze man seemed not to hear that. He switched off the analyzing device, replaced slides and cover, then started for the door, indicating the others should follow.

"Where to?" Ham questioned.

"The name of Sawyer Linnett Bonefelt, or Old Bonepicker, has cropped up a number of times," Doc Savage reminded. "We will see what we can learn about him."

As they entered a specially constructed speed elevator, built for Doc Savage's exclusive use, which dropped them to a private garage in the skyscraper basement, Monk mentioned a point upon which he evidently had decided convictions.

"Whoever scratched that message in the hack, tellin' us to go to the opera, knew in advance what was gonna happen," he said.

SAWYER LINNETT BONEFELT was listed in the local financial guides as a private banker; a short history of his career indicated he had started as a pawnbroker and a vender of bail bonds, had branched and grown, and was now a financial power. His specialty was buying up defunct corporations and manufacturing enterprises and breaking them into parts and selling them for what usually amounted to a profit. This had earned him his soubriquet of "Old Bonepicker." His financial rating was well up in the millions.

"A buzzard's way of making a living," Monk opined, one small eye cocked in Ham's direction. "Only worse thing I can think of is bein' a lawyer and livin' off people's troubles."

Ham, who was one of the most astute and sought-after attorneys in the country, maintained a cold silence.

The directory gave them Sawyer Linnett Bonefelt's address. This was a doorway, a very decrepit doorway, in a grimy and uninviting street in that section of the city which welfare workers liked to call the worst slum. One peculiar thing they noted at once. The entire block of buildings seemed to be unoccupied. The windows bore the grime deposit of months; some were boarded up.

They examined the door, found no bell button, and knocked; but there was no answer, nothing but the bumping echoes, faintly audible, of the knock inside. They waited for a time, then Doc Savage went to work on the lock with his picking kit. It surrendered shortly.

The hall beyond the door was bleak and uncarpeted, but clean. Opening to the right was a bare, miserable office, and on the left was a bedroom, equally unprepossessing.

Ham went over to the desk, opened the drawers and boldly riffled papers inside. He examined some closely.

"Jove!" he breathed in an awed tone. "These papers have to do with the breaking up and selling of a ten-million-dollar corporation. Imagine a fellow who does business like that using this place for an office!"

Doc ran a finger over the desk, and noted the deposit of dust on it.

"The desk does not seem to have been used for"—he paused and noted the tightness of the room against city grime—"two or three weeks."

They examined the bedroom. Nothing was there. At the back of the corridor, they found a door. Monk tried it.

"Feel's pretty solid," he offered.

Doc Savage tapped the panel, tested it with one of the lock-picking instruments which had a sharp point.

"Of armor plate steel," he decided.

Monk looked very surprised, said, "That's danged funny!" and stepped aside so that Doc could go to work on the lock. Once through the door—and the lock did not surrender as easily as had the other—they were in vastly different surroundings.

Carpet on the floor seemed an inch deep, and was of an expensive grade. The walls were paneled in walnut and some other wood which was a brilliant yellow in hue. The lighting was indirect, with no bulbs visible.

The homely Monk offered in a dry tone: "Old Bonepicker seems to be sort of a Jekyll and Hyde guy. He kept that miser's office and bedroom outside to impress people, and probably lived back here."

They advanced hurriedly toward the nearest door, only to stop as the panel opened.

"I beg pardon," said the man who had opened the door. "Just what are you doing here?"

He was rotund with a full, flushed face and hair which was rather splotchily white. He wore a resplendent butler's uniform.

"I am Mr. Bonefelt's butler," he stated further.

Doc Savage advanced. He rarely showed expression, except by design. He was smiling now.

The butler backed away, looking puzzled, and let them in, and under the brighter light apparently recognized the bronzed giant, for he started violently. But by that time, Monk and Ham were also inside. The servitor started to close the door.

"Wait." Doc Savage said.

The bronze man seized the door, which was almost closed, opened it again and addressed the apparently empty corridor.

"Come on in, guys," he said, and his tone was one in which one underworld denizen would address another.

"O. K.," said a coarse voice from out of thin air.

Monk and Ham were standing behind the butler, so that their starts of surprise fortunately went unnoticed. An instant later, they got control of themselves, realizing that Doc Savage was playing a game and using his excellent ability as a ventriloquist.

The butler was deceived completely. He jumped at conclusions of his own. A gusty sigh of relief escaped him.

"So Doc Savage throwed in with you, eh, boys?" he chuckled at what he apparently thought were invisible companions of the bronze man. "That's swell!"

Monk nearly choked.

"This guy knows something!" he howled. "Grab 'im!"

The butler saw he had been tricked. He pitched backward. Both hands fanned under his long, braided coat tails and came out with a pair of enormous army automatics. He did not use them. Doc Savage was upon him, gripping his wrists.

The guns whooped thunder, and their lead tore the rich carpet and split hardwood floorboards underneath. The man kicked, tried to bite. Doc Savage lifted him bodily, upset him, banged him down on the floor, and such was the shock that the man lost his weapons. Monk sat upon him.

"Glory be!" grinned the simian chemist. "We finally got somebody we can ask questions."

Ham unsheathed his sword cane and let the butler look closely at the long blade. He lifted a handkerchief from the prisoner's pocket and drew it across the blade: the linen square was cut through, a graphic illustration of just how sharp the fine steel sword was.

"Take his right ear first, Ham," Monk suggested. "I think it's a little bigger than the left."

Ham said, "An ear does not hurt. We will take an eye, because when you pull an eyeball out and begin to cut through the muscles behind it, it feels as if the whole brain was being hauled out."

"Aw, nuts!" said the prisoner. "I been through this third degree stuff before!"

Doc SAVAGE studied the man, then knelt and kneaded some of the fellow's joints in a manner which produced great pain. Doc noted the results carefully. He shook his head.

"Physical pain does not terrify this man," he said. "The fellow knows he can take only so much, then he will faint. Many criminals are that way."

Monk scowled. "Let's try it, anyhow."

Instead of replying, Doc Savage produced a small case little larger than a cigarette lighter, and from it drew a hypodermic needle with a transparent barrel. He charged it with a bright-green fluid from a magazine contained in the tiny case.

"Truth serum," he said. "The results are not always reliable, but the man will talk; and in the course of time we are certain to get at least a line on what we want to know."

The captive sneered.

"Bulls tried that on me once," he growled. "They didn't get a thing!"

"They did not try this kind," Doc assured him. "It is a concoction devised by myself and Monk, here."

The captive screamed as the serum was administered.

Monk bounced around on the prisoner's chest as the man sought vainly to arise and flee.

"How long?" the homely chemist queried.

"Five minutes, perhaps," Doc replied.

"The man's talk will be rambling, at times making no sense, but we may be able to pick out——"

THE bronze man hurtled to the left, then lunged wildly for the south wall. His eyes were fixed on a spot in the walnut paneling, a place where what seemed to be a knot graining in the wood, had opened, disclosing the black maw of a concealed peephole.

Red flame lashed out of the aperture. A lightning bolt seemed to crack in the room, so loud was the shot.

On the floor, the prisoner emitted a long, awful howl.

Monk toppled off the captive, rolled wildly after Doc. He, too, had seen the open peephole. The hidden gun whacked thunder again. Monk bawled, clawed at his chest. Mutilated lead, a bullet flattened against a bulletproof vest which Monk wore, fell to the carpet. Then Monk gained the wall.

Ham, moving as swiftly, was also against the wall, out of range.

"Stay there!" Doc Savage rapped.

The prisoner reared up on the floor. His chest was leaking a pencil-sized red stream. He groveled and tried to insert a finger in the bullet hole to plug it.

"They're croakin' me to shut me up!" he wailed.

Monk roared, "Now's your chance! Talk fast, guy!"

The wounded man screamed, "Go to the Spook's Nest!"

"The Spook's Nest?" Monk barked. "Where's that?"

"Marikan!" the man gulped. It's Marikan's place in the country. Get into the north tower and——"

The hidden gun banged again. The man's head jerked violently. The bullet must have been a dumdum, because bits of the head contents were carried out as it passed through, and the man fell over, dead.

Doc Savage was under the secret loophole now. It was of a size little more than sufficient to pass a gun snout. Doc thrust a hand into a pocket. The object he brought out might have been a steel ball bearing. He flipped it through the hole. Then he sprang away.

Monk and Ham lunged furiously to get clear. They had seen those things which resembled ball bearings used on other occasions. They were tiny grenades, incredibly violent.

There was a roar, a splintering of wood, a screeching of drawn nails—and most of the wall about the loophole caved in, admitting a cloud of dust and débris. This flooded across the floor, almost covering the prisoner who had been shot through the chest, then through the brain.

Doc Savage waded through the wreckage while it was still settling. He had covered his ears with his hands so that the concussion would not deafen him, and now he used both aural organs and eyes. He saw nothing. There was nobody inside the other room, which was narrow and apparently a bedroom.

He did hear footsteps. They were rapid, and in the rear somewhere. He raced in that direction.

He came to a dining room. One of the chairs had been upset and was still rocking on its rounded back portion. Doc went on, tried the door on the other side. It was locked. He crashed a fist against the panel. It split. He used a foot, and the panel fell out. He reached through and found a key in the other side and unlocked the door and passed through.

"You will explain yourself," said a deep, youthful voice.

IT was gloomy in the passage—which probably led to the

regions of the back door—and a brief instant elapsed before details became apparent.

Russel Wray, dark hair and white mustache making him seem slightly bizarre, was holding a long-barreled revolver which, unlike the blunt weapon he had wielded at the Easeman apartment, looked as long and lean as the man who held it.

Behind Wray stood Ada Easeman. In her capable right hand was Wray's stubby gun, of large calibre on a small frame. She still wore her emerald evening frock.

Doc Savage demanded, "Which one of you shot that man?"

They looked surprised, then they glanced at each other and strange expressions came upon their features. The girl spoke first.

"I didn't," she said. "We just came in and had separated to search the house. Then the shooting started, and that terrible explosion. We met here."

Doc Savage looked at Wray, said nothing.

"I never shot any one!" Wray snapped.

"Is there more than a back and a front door?" Doc asked.

"That is all," the girl said.

Ham ran into the corridor. His sword cane was unsheathed, but he showed no undue excitement.

"Monk is watching the front door," he advised.

"You take the back door," Doc told him. "We will search the house."

Ada Easeman interjected, "Wait! Do you know what this is all about?"

Doc Savage eyed her. "We are beginning to get an idea."

"Invisible men," she said.

The bronze man nodded. "Who is the brain behind the thing?"

The girl fingered the fabric of her evening gown absently. The tint of her nails blended perfectly with the emerald hue of the garment.

"That is what we want to know," she stated. "My father, P. Treve Easeman, and Sawyer Linnett Bonefelt were seized and made invisible by these men."

Doc exhibited no surprise. "Why?"

"Extortion," said the girl. "A flat sum of one million dollars in cash was demanded to make each of them visible again. Whatever the infernal process is, it seems that a man can be made invisible, then changed back to visibility again."

"Then what happened?" Doc Savage asked.

"They took father to Boston to hold him while he was invisible, so that he would be separated from Old Bonepicker—I mean, Mr. Bonefelt," explained Ada Easeman. "But my father managed to evade his guard, undiscovered, and telegraph you to get aboard the plane by which he was to be brought to New York City the next day."

From the region of the front door, Monk called, "There ain't no sign that the noise attracted any attention. Some people came out and looked, then went back in their houses. I guess nobody else lives in this block."

"Old Bonepicker owns the entire block and allows no one to live here, so that it will be quiet," said Russel Wray.

Doc directed the girl: "Go ahead with what happened in the plane."

"My father was writing a note on airplane stationery to get to you when some one opened a window and the note blew back and Telegraph Edmunds got it," she elaborated. "Telegraph read it, and it made him so mad that he shot my father. Here; I have the note."

She fished a folded paper from her gown and passed it over.

Doc Savage studied the missive without unfolding it. The paper was soiled and about of the size of the communication which Telegraph Edmunds and his men had examined beside the road near the airport. It was on Excelsior Airways stationery.

The unfinished writing read:

I, P. Treve Easeman, and another man, Sawyer Linnett Bonefelt, have been seized and made invisible by a gang of men. Telegraph Edmunds, seated behind me, is a lieutenant of the gang, but not the chief. I do not know the latter's identity.

This gang plans to extract a million dollars a piece from myself and Bonefelt for making us visible again. Then they are going to make themselves invisible and start a campaign of gigantic robberies. Their first crime, planned for tonight, will be robbery of the audience at the opera, and their second——

The writing ended there, evidently stopped when the gust of wind had come through the opened plane window.

Doc Savage asked, "Can you explain what happened at the airport?"

"I certainly can," the girl snapped. "My father had telephoned Bonefelt that he had enlisted your aid. You see, Bonefelt had escaped, and was at the airport. During the excitement, he followed Telegraph Edmunds and his men. It was he who snatched this note back again."

"Where was your father?"

"Wounded," said the young woman. "He managed to get out of the plane before Telegraph's men searched it, then crawled back inside and lay in one of the seats, unable to move. Your man Monk found him. Then Telegraph came, and during the fighting which followed, Russel, here, and myself, got my father away, aided by Old Bonepicker.

"Oh, yes, Old Bonepicker came to my apartment and got us. That was right after you told us to wait. I was so anxious to find my father that I neglected to tell you where we had gone."

The dapper Ham had heard the whole recital from where he was guarding the rear door. Now he expressed an opinion.

"Thin," he said, "very thin."

The girl and Russel Wray looked indignant.

"Where is your father now?" Doc Savage asked. "Where is this Old Bonepicker?"

"In a limousine in a garage out back," said the girl. "Maybe they're right here now, listening. You can't see them."

"We'll get them," Wray declared. "They can tell their own story."

"Just a moment," Doc Savage put in. "Who is Marikan?"

"Marikan?" the girl echoed blankly.

"I never heard of any one named Marikan," said Wray.

Chapter 10

INVISIBLE RAIDERS

Doc Savage withheld advice that the name Marikan had been uttered by the man recently slain, although both the girl and Wray showed curiosity on that point; but the bronze man spoke before they got around to voicing an inquiry.

"Go get the two invisible men, Easeman and Bonefelt," he suggested. "Bring them here."

"You might help us," Wray pointed out.

Doc Savage appeared not to hear the words, and made no reply. Wray frowned; his white mustache shifted as he nipped his upper lip, then he turned and walked past Ham and through the rear door. The girl followed.

Ham flicked his sword cane. "Should we watch them?"

Doc Savage said, "That killer is still somewhere on the premises, possibly."

"Sure it wasn't Wray or the girl?" Ham queried.

Again, Doc Savage did not answer. He moved back to the chamber where the little grenade had exploded and examined the dust which had settled on the floor; but this bore no footprints. The slayer had fled either before or immediately after the blast.

Doc gave attention to other doors and found some locked, others unlocked.

He was picking the lock on one of the doors when there was a sharp outcry in a strange voice.

"Help!" It was a man's voice. "She's killing me!"

Ham yelled from the door, "Doc! Something is happening out behind the house!"

Doc Savage was already in motion. He flung down a corridor, whipped past Ham, and was in a large garden which ran the entire length of the block.

The garden was a remarkable thing for the slum district, an affair of exquisite taste and beauty. The overhead area was glassed in, the transparent panels arranged so they could be swung back mechanically, and there was a hot-house system of steam pipes. There were many rare tropical plants in bloom.

"Help!" bawled the strange male voice—"Help!"

The cries were coming from the south end of the garden, where there was an arched door. The bronze man raced past a glass case in which orchids were growing, and reached the door and dived inside.

"Help!" squalled the voice.

The shouting man lay on his back. He was handcuffed wrist and ankle. A swarthy man, he had big ears, a tremendous nose, a small mouth, and the rest of him was plump. His neat blue suit bulged a little with fat.

Over him crouchd the girl, Ada Easeman. She was threatening him with the stubby gun. The stare which she directed at Doc Savage was hard to fathom.

"It's a trick!" she snapped. "This man tried to seize me, even though he is handcuffed."

The dark man squawled, "What a liar she is! The hussy! It is ready to kill me, she was!"

"That is not true!" Ada Easeman gritted.

"Who is he?" Doc demanded.

The girl shook her head. "I never saw him before."

"The lying hussy!" the handcuffed man yelled. "She knows me well!"

"Your name?" Doc said quietly.

"Marikan," the man barked—"Angus Angelo Marikan!"

RUSSEL WRAY appeared, racing from somewhere in the depths of the building, flourishing his long gun, demanding, "What on earth is happening?"

"Let me have your gun," Doc Savage requested.

Wray puckered a frown around his white mustache and thought that over. His facial expression was not hard to read. He decided not to surrender his weapon.

Doc Savage seemed prepared for no sudden movement, but he changed position, doing it so swiftly that his motions were a trifle blurred. Wray grunted loudly and tried to do something in defense with his gun, but was far too slow. Doc got one metallic hand on the long gun. They scuffled. Wray barked once in pain, then spun completely around and upset. He had lost his gun.

"Good, very good!" Marikan clashed his manacle links together in getting unsteadily erect. "They are working together, these two."

"He's crazy!" snapped Wray. "Loony!"

Marikan tried to wave his arms, but the handcuffs prevented the movement.

"Half an hour ago they seize me, handcuff me and put rags and stuff in my mouth!" he shouted. "They leave me. They are crooks!"

The girl jutted her stubby gun.

"You stop those lies!" she rapped.

She did not see Doc Savage until the bronze man was at her side. Doc got the gun out of her fingers with a deft whipping motion which left her staring, surprised, at her empty hand.

The bronze man now examined both the girl's gun and that of Wray's. He broke them, scrutinized the cartridges in the cylinders and found both fully loaded, with no empty cartridges. Both barrels were clean, oily.

"That proves we did not shoot the man inside!" the girl said angrily.

Marikan rasped handcuff links and howled, "Nothing, it proves! Nothing! The girl had another gun. I saw it, I truly did. It was a big gun, and she carried it in an emerald hand bag. You know—a hand bag what is green."

The girl whitened, and grated, "Everything he says is a lie!"

"I see her hide something in the garden!" Marikan bellowed triumphantly. "Maybe it was the gun! I show you."

Doc Savage studied the girl. "Did you have such a bag?"

She hesitated, snapped, "You wouldn't believe me!"

"I show you!" Marikan howled triumphantly.

He led the way out in the garden, to a spot which was visible from the door, and began to peer around.

"It was here, somewhere," he said. "Truly, it was!"

Doc Savage searched. Nowhere did the rich black earth in the plant boxes show traces of recent disturbance. Then he lifted a fallen tropical leaf. He dug in.

The gun which he brought out was blue, of large calibre, and the discharged cartridges exactly matched in number the shots which had been fired inside the house.

The weapon was encased in an evening bag, a large one, of an emerald green hue which exactly matched the color of the girl's evening frock.

"Your bag?" Doc asked.

Her nod was sharp, enraged. "Yes."

With a pocket lens, the bronze man studied the gun. He saw no finger prints, but did discern smears which indicated they had been wiped off.

Then, quite unexpectedly, the gun and bag were wrenched from his hands.

It was one of the rare occasions when the bronze man was taken completely off guard. Such was the shock that he stood a moment, held stationary by surprise.

"Look!" Marikan screamed. "The gun, it is floating in the air!"

He sounded beside himself with horror.

As if the shout had switched off the spell, Doc Savage lunged for the gun. Both arms were out, clutching. Then came a flash. Varicolored lights exploded in his eyeballs. He had been struck a terrific blow in the face.

"Run for it!" said a voice.

It was an invisible man, and Doc Savage had heard the voice before. Coarse, aged, querulous! It had been on the voice recorder planted in the P. Treve Easeman apartment. Old Bonepicker speaking.

The venerable tones were deceptive as to source, but Doc Savage lunged, still half blinded by the agony of the smash in the face, endeavoring to seize the unseen speaker. He encountered no one, and was not greatly surprised.

The girl and Wray both whirled, ran.

Doc Savage leaped to stop them. Something he could not see got between his legs, and he tripped and went down. There was the agony of a second terrific smash on his head. Dazed, for all of his fortitude, he rolled to one side.

Marikan was jumping up and down, clashing his cuff links and howling.

"Crazy, I must be!" he screamed. "Something you no can see, she in here!"

Then there was a smack; Marikan's nose flattened, then shaped out again and began to stream scarlet as he fell. The invisible attacker—attackers if there were more then one—had felled him. He groveled, bellowing incoherently in very erratic English.

The girl and Wray were out of sight. Monk and Ham came charging through the garden from the other part of the slum labyrinth which seemed to be Old Bonepicker's home. Both were excited, anxious for a fight.

The gun which had been seized from Doc, and the other guns, were gone. Either the girl or Wray must have borne them off in the excitement.

In the direction which the fugitives had taken, an automobile engine began moaning. Doc Savage heaved up and made for the sound. So dazed was he by the blows that Monk and Ham kept up with him and even drew ahead, something they could not ordinarily have done.

They entered a large garage which held an expensive limousine and two large coupes; and over in the corner a black, rich town car. The door to the street was open. Doc lurched to it.

A car—it looked like the same phæton which the girl and Wray had used at the airport, although the top was now up—heeled around a corner at the end of the block. Its roar receded.

There was no other vehicle in sight.

Marikan came up howling. "They're the crooks, the whole lot!"

DOC SAVAGE did not attempt to reach his own machine, knowing the limitations of pursuit through the gloomy city streets. He closed the garage door, found there was a lock on the inside, and secured it.

"They're the crooks!" Marikan howled.

Monk scowled at him. "And who are you?"

"Me?" Marikan tried to spread his hands, but was hampered by the handcuffs. "Me? I am the chiropractor."

"The what?" Monk's scowl darkened.

"I doctor the chiropractor way," explained the other, and tried to wave his arms. He almost lost his balance on his linked ankles, and barely missed upsetting. "When somebody, he feel the pain, I push and pull the spine, and he get well." He snapped fingers. "Just like that!"

Monk kept his scowl. "What are you doing here?"

"This man, Sawyer Linnett Bonefelt, the one they call Old Bonepicker, he have take treatments and owe me the bill," explained Marikan. "I come here to collect. Boy, do I get in mess! That girl in green dress, and that man with black hair and white mustache, they grab me——"

"Why?" Monk interjected.

Marikan shrugged, almost fell again.

"How I know?" he snorted. "They do not want me prowl around, I guess."

"How did you get in?" Monk quizzed.

"A key, Old Bonepicker give to me," Marikan explained.

He fished in a pocket with some difficulty, and brought out a rather massive key.

"You see, it is often I come to treat Old Bonepicker," he elaborated. "It is custom for me to just walk right in."

Monk glanced at Doc Savage.

"What do you think, Doc?" questioned the homely chemist. "Did that girl and Wray kill the man inside to shut his mouth?"

Ham clipped, "The dying man mentioned this fellow Marikan, under suspicious circumstances."

"That's right!" Monk exploded. He glared at Marikan. "What's the Spook's Nest?"

Marikan blew on a wrist which the manacles had chafed.

"It is my skunk farm you talk about, maybe?" he grunted.

"Your what?" Monk gulped.

"My place where the skunk, she is raise," Marikan replied. "You know him, the fur farm. I raise skunks. Nobody is ever come around because the place, she smell bad. So I call her my Spook's Nest."

"This thing sure has its angles," Monk grinned.

Inside the house, a telephone started ringing.

THE phone had hardly stopped ringing when Doc Savage was racing toward the instrument. He found it in one of the sumptuously furnished rooms near where he had encountered the girl and Wray. He lifted the receiver.

It was with Old Bonepicker's aged, querulous tones that the bronze man spoke, and in the exactness of the imitation was an indication of just how perfectly he had mastered the art of voice mimicry.

The tone which came from the other end of the wire was harsh, surprised, but identifiable. It was Telegraph Edmunds.

"What the heck?" he rapped. "You there, Bonepicker?"

"What do you think?" Doc parried in Old Bonepicker's voice.

"Does Doc Savage suspect Ada Easeman and Wray being mixed in with us?" Telegraph demanded.

Doc replied, "That is hard to say."

"Well, we oughta know, because the girl and Wray can

do us a lot of good if Doc Savage don't suspect them and they can get to working with him," Telegraph stated. "Now, about this Federated Payroll matter. It's all set for eight o'clock this morning."

"What is the plan?" Doc asked in his assumed tone.

"Just what we figured on," said Telegraph. "I just thought I'd give you the lowdown. There ain't a chance of a slip."

Then he hung up.

Monk and Ham came in, Marikan trailing them with a series of awkward leaps that got him along at a fair rate in spite of his braceleted ankles.

Doc Savage asked him, "Did Old Bonepicker ever go to your Spook's Nest fur ranch?"

Marikan nodded. "Sure, he did."

"Why?"

"Old Bonepicker, he help pay for her," Marikan explained. "Then the old Shylock, he say he take it away from me because I can no pay interest."

"We going out there?" Monk demanded.

"Yes," Doc said. "But first, we are going to be on hand at the Federated Payroll offices, where something seems to be set for eight o'clock."

Chapter 11

GHOST PRINTS

FEDERATED PAYROLL was a product of the complexity of the modern business world. They took contracts from factories and large business establishments, whereby they agreed to handle payrolls—getting the money, taking it to their offices, having their own accountants apportion it in small envelopes bearing the names of workmen. Then armored cars carried the envelopes to the respective places of employment, where armed attendants distributed the wages.

The payrolls were made up in the morning, and it was not unusual for a large sum of money to be on hand.

The clock on the car dash stood a fractional bit back of eight when Doc Savage, Monk, Ham and Marikan pulled up before Federated Payroll. The sun had brought a swelter of fog in rising, and the air felt damp and cloying, although sidewalks were dry.

Two uniformed guards eyed closely Doc Savage's party as

they entered the establishment. They were to remember that later.

There was a flight of stairs, closed at the bottom by iron gates which were now open, and beside which other guards stood. At the top of the stairs was a waiting room enclosed by a metal grille, and beyond that, the enormous room in which the payrolls were made up.

At each end of this room, high up, was an armor plate pillbox with machine gunners posted inside. Federated Payroll took few chances.

Doc Savage stepped into the barred anteroom. It was like a signal—there came a howl from one of the pillboxes. The next instant, a guard toppled out. From that distance, it looked as if the entire top of his head had been caved in.

Stenographers shrieked. A man sprang for an alarm button. There was the noise of a blow, and he fell. Tumult seized the room. The other machine gunner toppled out of the other armored pillbox.

A large pile of greenbacks slid off a table and piled up in mid-air below, as if they had been scooped into an invisible sack.

"The invisible men!" Monk bawled.

Another pile of greenbacks lifted, as if they had become lighter than air, and drifted along an aisle. Two girls looked at them and fainted.

Monk howled, "What'll we do?"

"Block the exits, you missing link!" Ham told him.

Doc Savage rapped, "Get under cover!"

Monk eyed the bronze man. It was the first time he could recall having seen his chief sidestep a fight. Monk often suspected that Doc liked a scrap better than any of them, and that sort of excitement was the spice of life to himself and Ham.

"We've tried to fight these invisible men before with ordinary methods, and had no luck," Doc said rapidly. "The thing to do is play safe until we can cope with them."

Saying that, the bronze man swept Monk, Ham and Marikan back through the door.

Marikan jumped up and down and stuttered, "Awful, I call it! Awful!"

Two or three of the head clerks were yelling commands and a guard was dashing about waving his gun, but their attempts to bring order were completely lost in the chaos. Now and then, a clerk would fall to the accompaniment of a grisly blow. It was evident that some of these men were being killed.

Money was jumping off desks and out of sacks and strong boxes and floating away. Seeing that, even the men became hysterical. It was too uncanny for quick comprehension.

On the chief clerk's desk, a bottle of ink was upset by one of the invisible beings. The clerk stared, eyes popping, as he saw what looked to him like a splash in the ink, as if a hand had dropped in it; then a series of black finger prints appeared on the desk.

The clerk could see the ink clinging to the invisible fingers. Then the owner of the transparent fingers wiped them on the desk blotter and threw the blotter at the clerk. The clerk shrieked as if the entire earth had been hurled at him. That gave him an idea.

"Throw ink on the things!" he howled.

No one heard him. The uproar was deafening. One of the guards had turned loose senselessly with a machine gun.

Doc Savage and his party got to the foot of the stairs and closed the barred gate.

"Use tear gas," he ordered the guards there.

But they wanted to know what was going on. The result was an argument, and in the midst of it there was a shout from a man around the corner, on a side street. They ran out. The one who had shouted was a pedestrian.

"Money!" he squawled. "A million dollars! It came out of that window and went floating down the street!"

Doc Savage glanced at the window. It gave admittance to the payroll concern, and the bars had been shoved aside. One of the invisible men must have walked into the establishment earlier and loosened the rods.

Trailed by his party, Doc ran in the direction which the money had taken. He found nothing—which was about what he had expected. There were alleys, side streets and a score of doorways into which the invisible raiders could have ducked.

"Most incredible thing I ever heard of!" Marikan gulped. "And you think my polecat farm, she might have something to do with her?"

Monk roared, "It'd better have! If we don't stop these spook guys, they'll rob the country blind! Man, they've got the world by the tail!"

Police sirens were howling.

Doc said, "Come."

"You go to my polecat farm?" Marikan demanded.

"We do," said the bronze man.

BACK in the offices of Federated Payroll, the excitement was accentuated rather than calmed by the arrival of squads of puzzled policemen and detectives. These bustled about, few of them believing what they were told, despite the occurrence of a kindred calamity at the opera the night before.

Finger print experts arrived and went to work. They were not long in finding the prints on the chief clerk's desk, and they photographed them from many angles.

"Those are prints of one of the invisible men," the clerk insisted, and told about the blotter being thrown at him.

Within a quarter of an hour, the prints had been rushed to the police department and identified. There was a new burst of excitement. Every one of the police broadcasting stations went into operation.

Doc Savage had a radio in his car, and it was tuned to the police band. He wanted news of the invisible-man robber, and he got plenty.

The police announcer was so excited he could hardly speak.

"Urgent to all cars!" he said rapidly. "Finger print identification of one of invisible-man robbers. Print was found on desk in payroll company office. It was traced. It is the print of Doc Savage, whose prints were on file in connection with a special commission which he holds on New York police force. Arrest and hold this man for questioning. He was seen by Federated Payroll guards at the scene of crime."

"Ah," Monk said sourly. "Do we all stand up and cheer?"

"Cheer!" Marikan stuttered. "Very extremely bad, I call it. You should cheer, I ask you?"

"That is just the missing link's way of saying he is dumfounded," Ham put in dryly.

Monk was driving. He took his hands off the wheel to wave his arms.

"But how'd Doc's prints get on a desk?" he yelled. "We weren't even in the part of the office where the desks are."

Traveling near seventy, the car angled hungrily for the edge of the pavement.

"Watch your driving!" Ham screamed.

When the machine was straightened out again, Doc Savage spoke. His remarkable voice still maintained its tranquillity, and he showed by no visible mannerism that he had just heard anything of significance.

"Remember when I was unconscious at the opera?" he asked.

"Do I?" Monk snorted.

"Examining my fingers later, I found traces of wax—as I told you," Doc reminded. "That wax means my finger print impressions were taken. From those molds, it would be simple to make castings with some flexible stuff which they then made invisible. With these, my finger prints were planted on the desk."

"Jove!" Ham bent his sword cane thoughtfully. "They have confidence. They picked you for their fall guy, if I may resort to slang."

Chapter 12

FUR FARM

MARIKAN'S rural establishment for the propagation of skunks proved to be well down the New Jersey coast, which was a help, since it was situated in a different State.

Nevertheless, Doc Savage carefully avoided the main highways, and got out of sight below the doors when they passed cars, especially after he heard the stations of the Newark and Jersey City police radioing his description and a pickup order.

The police radio broadcast brought the information that no less than seven persons had been killed by head blows during the raid of the invisible men upon the payroll firm. The license numerals of Doc Savage's car were given, together with a description of its body style and color.

"It'd be tough if we were picked up," Monk stated. "Maybe we'd better change cars."

"At least, we should change the identity of this one," Doc Savage agreed.

Monk stopped the car in a deserted-looking spot, and the bronze man drew from the tool compartment an extra set of license plates for each of the States bounding New York. He selected a pair for New Jersey and substituted them for the tabs which the car already bore. Out of the tool compartment came a contrivance which resembled an ordinary hand sprayer.

"Those Jersey tags under your name?" Monk questioned.

"No," Doc told him. "They were issued to a second-hand car which was run into the ocean after the new plates were removed."

The bronze man now turned the sprayer on the car and began working the pump handle. This threw a cloud of almost colorless material over the machine. The stuff had a biting tang that set Monk and Ham coughing. The color of the car had been a somber black. Now it changed, becoming a rather light and cheap gray tint.

"Chemical bleach," the bronze man explained. "Much quicker than repainting."

The entire car had changed color when they again entered it and drove on.

An airplane droned in the sky in the direction of New York City. Monk thrust his hand out, then yanked it back, grunting, "That might be a police plane," and used the rear-view mirror, which he wrenched from its anchorage, to observe the aircraft.

"Funny," he said finally.

"What is?" Ham snapped.

"I'll swear that plane took a distinct swing to avoid passing overhead," advised the homely chemist.

"Imagination," Ham jeered.

"Maybe," Monk admitted. "But it looked like they didn't want anybody to look 'em over too closely."

Doc Savage asked Marikan, "In just what direction does your fur farm lie?"

The big-nosed man pointed. "There, long way."

The bronze man watched the plane which Monk had observed, noting particularly the direction which it took, and the others in the car caught the significance of what he was doing, and also scrutinized the craft. It was a seaplane, they noted.

"Son of my gun!" Marikan exclaimed. "That bird, she go over by direction of my cat farm!"

THE fur farm was situated on marshland—rather, on a bit of highland in a considerable area of marsh, and there were no neighbors within some two miles.

"The swamp, she have no bottom," Marikan advised. "No can build her a house on the mud or she jump right up and sink out of sight."

Cutting very close to the mound on which the fur farm stood was a stream of no great depth but for some width—a salt water tidal creek. This chanced to run straight and closely resembled a canal—it probably had been dredged at some time in the past, for the banks gave evidence of being somewhat higher, and supported a growth of rather stunted trees.

On the stream, hidden by the trees, rested four seaplanes. They were not large craft, all being single-motored, capable of carrying no more than eight or ten persons at the most. Among them was the ship which Monk had observed.

"I'm son of my gun!" gulped Marikan. "What all this stuff, she mean?"

"You sure you don't know?" Monk demanded sourly.

Marikan waved his arms and looked vastly injured.

"If I know something she is phony, would I bring you out?" he asked.

"Yeah," Monk agreed. "That's so, too."

They had parked the car a long distance back, under a tree where it was hidden from the air. They had gone on foot, stooping low in the salt grass, crawling at times, wading more often. When they made out the planes, Doc Savage stopped.

"There is something going on," he said slowly. "Ham, you and Marikan wait here. Monk and I will go on."

"Can't we go together?" demanded Ham, who disliked to miss the possible excitement.

"No telling what will happen to us," Doc advised him. "Should it be necessary, some one had best be in the clear, to get hold of the other members of our crowd and set them to work on the thing."

Ham nodded. The other members of Doc Savage's organization—Colonel John "Renny" Renwick, a famous engineer; William Harper "Johnny" Littlejohn, a renowned archæologist, and Major Thomas J. "Long Tom" Roberts, an electrical engineer who was considered a wizard—were not at present in New York, but scattered, the engineer and the electrical expert in Europe, and the archæologist in the western part of the United States, investigating a new cliff dwelling discovery.

Doc Savage went on, Monk trailing him closely. Because they found it was going to be necessary to wade a small lake, they removed most of their outer clothing. It was very chilly. The fog which had characterized the earlier morning hours had almost vanished.

They reached a point where they could discern activity about the planes. Men, well-dressed, intelligent-looking fellows who, nevertheless, conveyed the impression of being hard and unscrupulous, were transferring bags and satchels from the planes.

Numerous bags and satchels were coming out of the planes of their own accord and floating ashore, obviously carried by invisible men.

"Their headquarters!" Monk whispered.

The homely chemist wheeled and pushed his pet pig, Habeas Corpus, down on his haunches, advising in a whisper, "You stick here, Habeas."

The shote obeyed like a well-trained dog.

HAM, watching with binoculars, managed to keep fairly close track of Doc and Monk. Marikan lay beside Ham and muttered under his breath.

"I like this a whole lot, you can say I don't," Marikan mumbled.

"Be silent, please," Ham requested shortly.

Marikan gave another opinion, but it was too low to be heard. Then the man fell silent, and the only noise was that of the breeze in the marsh grass and an occasional cry from one of the gang unloading the planes—taking off the loot of their opera and payroll forays, no doubt. Otherwise, there was very little sound. Then Marikan grunted.

Marikan's grunt was loud. It was also strange. Ham spun over—they were lying prone—and eyed his companion. Marikan was lying very motionless, and his face was jammed into the soft swamp mire in such a manner that it was doubtful if he was breathing.

Ham opened his mouth. He did not intend to shout. Rather, the mouth opening was a surprise reaction. Ham regretted the unconscious act an instant later. Something jammed into his gaping mouth. It felt like cloth—but it was invisible.

Ham hacked, gagged. He reached for the unseen obstruction. His arms were gripped by unseen forces. He kicked. Ponderous, unseen weights seemed to attach themselves to his legs.

"Take her easy, dude," a voice advised. "You were suckers to think you could walk up on this place. Why, we've got invisible men standing along all of the roads! We've got our men in the police stations, listening to every word that is said!"

Ham threw back his head and made as loud a noise as he could through his nose. His best effort might have been heard a hundred yards away. Doc Savage was already far beyond that distance.

Croaking sounds of pain escaped Ham as something he could not see, probably a finger, jabbed into his left eye.

"Keep quiet or you'll lose the lamp!" he was directed.

Marikan now turned over, the grotesqueness of the motion showing that the invisible men were doing the shifting. His mouth came open and swamp dirt jumped out, apparently under the prying of an unseen finger.

"He's only unconscious," said another of the invisible men. "What'll we do with them?"

"Hold them here a while, until Doc Savage and the other one are taken," said another unseen speaker. "Then we will see what reaction a particle of lead of a predetermined size, say .38 calibre, has on their mental processes. It ought to be an interesting study."

Ham said nothing. Ordinarily, he did not become scared or greatly unnerved, but now he felt as if he were being showered with dry ice and was receiving a series of electrical shocks. It was his closest encounter with the invisible men, and the unearthly strangeness of it was appalling. Moreover, the invisible men knew Doc Savage and Monk had gone on, and were probably closing in on the pair now.

DOC SAVAGE and Monk were very close to the fur farm. The establishment consisted of a battery of wire pens with an unpleasant odor, and two long, ramshackle stuccoed buildings, one of which was open at the sides and obviously intended for the harvesting of the crop, the skinning of the animals and the curing of the hides. There was also a section devoted to the storing of food for the fur bearers.

It was into the larger building, probably a dwelling, that the men and their invisible associates were bearing the loot.

Monk said, "Maybe I oughta brought Habeas along. You know, he——"

The pig trotted up.

Monk scowled at the shote admonishingly.

"I told you to stay behind," he breathed. "Haven't I got you trained so——"

He fell silent. His small eyes widened as they scrutinized the homely porker. Habeas seemed uneasy. Oversize ears were distended. He roved his head from side to side.

Monk looked at Doc Savage. "Invisible men!" he growled.

"So it would seem," Doc whispered back.

They were keeping their tones down so that they barely carried to each other, and now Monk gave Habeas a shove.

"Where are they?" he whispered. "Smell 'em out, hog!"

Not for nothing had Monk expended most of his spare time over a period of years in training Habeas, who, due to the hardships of a youth spent in deserty Arabia, showed no signs of growing beyond the stature of a small pig. Habeas moved away slowly, plainly with reluctance. A moment later, he was pointing, after the fashion of a hunting dog.

"Swell!" Monk whispered. "An invisible man over there!"

But Doc Savage shook his head, watching the pig.

"Not so good," he said. "The invisible man seems to be following our trail through the marsh grass."

Monk gulped, "Blazes! How we gonna get the guy? We can't tell where he is!"

Doc Savage did not reply, but watched Habeas Corpus instead. The pig was now in something of a welter of excitement. He pointed a different direction, then shifted his attention. He crouched down and scuttled back to Doc and Monk, fear in his every movement.

"Surrounded!" Doc Savage said grimly. "They have been watching us the whole time!"

Monk snaked a supermachine pistol from its holster. The mechanism of the gun, the mercy bullets, were both impervious to moisture.

Doc Savage directed, "Get set! Things are going to break!"

Monk gave Habeas a shove.

"Beat it, hog," he directed. "This ain't gonna be no place for you!"

Chapter 13

ALCHEMY

Doc Savage still wore a vest of peculiar construction. It consisted of a bulletproof outer covering, and, under that, numerous pockets, padded and tailored in place so that, in wearing the vest, the bronze man's proportions were increased only slightly.

The pockets held innumerable devices, the scientific gadgets with which Doc Savage chose to fight, rather than with more prosaic firearms.

The vest pockets yielded up several small grenades of varying color. There were tiny detonating levers on these. Doc actuated the levers, then hurled the missiles away—one to the right, another to the left, a third behind them, and a series ahead, progressing toward the two buildings.

The grenades burst and spewed an astounding quantity of smoke that looked some degrees blacker than drawing ink. The pall spread. The whole vicinity became blanketed with intense sepia.

The pig, Habeas Corpus, ran away, grunting loudly and taking tremendous leaps.

Doc Savage said, "I'm down, Monk—out of your way!"

Monk grunted and held his machine pistol to his side, latched the firing lever back and pivoted, spraying a storm of mercy bullets at the height of an average man's waist. Pained howls indicated the barrage had some effect.

Doc Savage clipped, "Enough!" and came to his feet when Monk ceased firing. He was less than an arm's length from the homely chemist, but could not see him. He found Monk by touch. They retreated.

Monk tried to make for the shed, but Doc guided him to the left, toward the house.

"But they're all in there," Monk gulped.

Doc did not answer. He threw more of the smoke grenades. He added four tear gas missiles, and others containing a gas which produced quick unconsciousness. He hurled these far enough away that they would not affect himself and Monk, for they had no masks.

They reached the house. The smoke had penetrated the dwelling. Inside was a black, howling bedlam.

Telegraph Edmunds's voice was bawling orders.

"Watch the marsh around the place!" he squawled. "Watch it close! They can't keep up this smoke very long. Then we'll get them!"

Doc Savage pushed Monk down.

"Wait here," he breathed.

The bronze man whipped in the direction of the creek where the seaplanes were moored. He could hear others running near by, obeying Telegraph's orders, spreading to watch the marsh.

The smoke pall did not extend as far as the planes, and Doc Savage, peering through scrawny brush, could see an armed man standing on a pontoon, watching intently. Escape by that route was manifestly impossible.

"You in the black plane!" Doc called.

There was only one black ship, the other three being a more common yellow. The pilot was standing on the left pontoon, holding a submachine gun. He started at the sound of the voice.

"Yeah, boss!" he replied.

Doc Savage had used a tone, the inflection and delivery so closely approximating the voice of Telegraph Edmunds that only with the two side by side, speaking alternately while being compared closely, could a difference have been detected.

"Take your ship and fly back to the place where you picked up the last load," Doc directed.

It was a long chance. The pilot hesitated.

"What about this mess here?" he demanded.

"We'll handle it," Doc said in Telegraph Edmunds's voice. "You circle around overhead until the smoke blows away, and if you don't see them running off over the marsh, go on away."

That seemed rational to the flier.

"O. K.," he agreed, and clambered into the cockpit.

Doc Savage eased back and, a moment later, heard the

plane engine start and knew from the manner in which the roar receded that the flier had taxied down the creek and was taking to the air.

DEPARTURE of the plane brought fresh uproar from the fur farm. Telegraph Edmunds dashed to the creek bank, glared at the plane, which was now in the air, and indulged in a species of spasm. His face was blue before he stopped cursing.

"They got away in that plane!" he bawled.

The plane came buzzing back, and was greeted with a fussillade of bullets. The smoke had not yet dissipated and the pilot made the mistake of thinking Doc Savage and his men were doing the shooting. He merely banked farther away and circled lazily, watching the marsh to see that no one fled. Thus, he was too distant to make out the mad arm-waving of Telegraph Edmunds.

It dawned on Telegraph that other planes were at hand for a pursuit. He ordered them in the air.

Running toward the ships, Telegraph's men came upon one of their number—not an invisible man—lying uncon-scious. He seemed to have been hit on the jaw. His gun was gone.

They reached the creek, stared at it, and Telegraph per-mitted himself another fit of rage. Gasoline, glistening with all the rainbow hues, was covering the creek waters, leaking from the tanks of the planes, through bullet holes.

Telegraph failed to even suspect that Doc Savage had seized the gun and shot holes in the fuel tanks during the firing at the ship which was in the air, thus blocking pursuit.

The breeze finally stirred the smoke and pushed it away, and since the little grenades had ceased to pour out the black pall, the air cleared.

Monk and Doc Savage were inside the house, which was untenanted except for themselves, excitement having drawn all others outdoors.

Monk was not exactly satisfied.

"Wish we was in that plane," he muttered. "They ain't gonna like it when they find us in here."

Belying the danger of their position, the apish chemist wore a wide, somehow rather cherubic grin. The same grin he had been known to wear on certain other occasions when the chances of his living more than a few minutes had seemed negligible. Monk was a rare type of individual. He seemed unable to conceive of such a thing as danger.

Doc Savage was glancing about the house. There was a bedroom, dining room, living room and kitchen, all poorly furnished. He opened closet doors, looked in the cupboard.

"That is strange," he said.

"The whole thing is strange," Monk agreed.

"The loot they were carrying in is nowhere in sight," Doc pointed out.

Monk lost his grin, began to circle the rooms and examine the walls. He was very careful to keep out of range of the windows. Telegraph Edmunds and his crew thought Doc and Monk had escaped in the plane, hence it had not occurred to them to look inside.

Doc Savage joined Monk in the hunt. The stove which stood in the living room was a round-bellied affair on a metal floor protector.

Peering closely, the bronze man noted one leg of the stove seemed brighter than the rest, as if from handling. He grasped it. His fingers found a catch concealed in the concave rear of the leg. He pressed the catch. A mechanism clicked, and stove and floor protector lifted and swung to one side.

"Well, well," Monk breathed. "Secrets and everything!"

THE hole they had exposed was large enough to pass a man comfortably, and the ladder had wide rungs and a hand rail. Doc Savage scrutinized the top of the ladder. He did not descend on the rungs, but swung and dropped some ten feet to the floor of a concrete passage and examined the foot of the ladder. There was no hidden alarm wiring guarding it.

"All right," he whispered, and Monk came down.

The mechanism for closing the unique stove-trapdoor was convenient and easily solved. Darkness clamped down when it was closed. Doc Savage still carried the generator-operated flashlights which they had employed during the night; these, being waterproof, still functioned.

Flash beams disclosed a sloping passage, which they traversed, coming to a door of steel—sheeted on the inside with lead, they discovered in passing through. It was closed when they found it, so they closed it behind them.

They were now in a room which hummed faintly, as if from machinery, and where the air smelled somewhat like that inside large generator power plants. At intervals there was a burst of brittle crackling, as if glass were being broken by large pailfuls. The walls, floor and ceiling were enameled a sanitary white.

"Maybe there's a back door to this dump," Monk offered.

Doc Savage made no comment, had no time to speak, in fact, before they heard voices ahead, sounds which indicated that men were approaching. It was the first hint that the subterranean labyrinth was tenanted.

There was a door to the right, manifestly not the one through which voices were coming, and Doc and Monk whipped for it, got it open and eased through into a passage.

Opening off the passage were various small niches, some of which held stores. Both men eased into a niche which held barrels and a tarpaulin covering. They sheltered themselves with the canvas.

Before many moments, there was a bustle in the other rooms. Men filed down from the surface, muttering and excited. Then Telegraph Edmunds put in an appearance, and his shouted orders were audible.

"Snap it up!" he commanded. "We've got to change our schedule and rush it through. This Doc Savage will spread an alarm. We haven't much time!"

Monk sucked in breath as the door of their passage opened. Men began to file through. The lights were not turned on and they were indistinct figures in the gloom.

The first of the parade passed; then another and another. Their breathing was noisy. That might indicate they were worried. Almost a dozen filed along. Then Telegraph Edmunds appeared at the entrance.

"Hep, hep!" he barked. "Make it snappy! I'll take a flashlight and go through these stores in this passage and see if there's anything that should be removed. Then I'll follow the rest of you. And you birds be careful about showing lights."

Doc Savage and Monk exchanged nudges in the darkness.

"We will have to take the chance," the bronze man decided.

They arose boldly and joined the procession. It was not an especially courageous course, and it was not remarkable that they did it without being discovered. The men were going fast, crowding each other, and it was dark. Doc got into line ahead of Monk, and they went forward rapidly.

They came to a room in which there was considerable activity. Some seconds elapsed before they realized what was happening there.

"Be sure to remove every stitch of clothing," said a voice. "That includes wrist watches, rings—and false teeth, if any. Remember that the presence of the slightest bit of metal on the body is liable to have fatal consequences."

Monk found Doc's ear—he could tell the finer texture of the bronze man's skin by touch—and whispered, "What do we do?"

"Do as they do," Doc decided. "Shed your clothing."

"I don't like this a lot," Monk advised, but complied with the suggestion.

Within a few moments, a peculiar prickling sensation became noticeable. It made itself apparent, first, about the eyes and nostrils and other tender parts of the body, then spread all over.

"Whew!" somebody complained. "I must have the itch!"

The voice which had given orders, said, "You are being exposed to the first conditioning rays in this room. This treatment brings about an oxidizing reaction which is quite necessary."

Some time passed, and it seemed that every one had removed clothing, for the room was comparatively quiet except for breathing and the rasp of finger nails on skin as somebody scratched himself.

"You have been here ten minutes," said the commanding voice. "You will now file out the door to your left. You have been instructed what to do."

Monk and Ham followed the crowd, jostled along, and found themselves shoved through a small door. They heard a series of long brushing noises, but failed to recognize the significance of that until they were propelled by the crush of bodies behind over a small rise in the floor.

Beyond was a steeply sloping chute. They slammed headlong down this and landed in a vat of some liquid which felt smooth and creamy. They made a large splash, and men cursed them.

"What is it?" demanded the voice of the director sharply.

"Some fool fell down the chute," another replied.

"That's all right," said the first. "Take long breaths and duck below the surface. It is essential that this compound cover every exposed inch of your body."

By the noises, Doc and Monk decided that the men were paddling across the tank, whatever it was, and clambering out on the opposite side. They followed suit.

They heard a man yell ahead. An instant later they knew the reason, for a fine spray of some chemical concoction struck their bodies, and the effect was very much as if hot lead had been poured upon them. They followed the others and dashed through the spray with all speed possible.

The darkness was profound and showed no signs of abating. The voice explained the reason for this.

"It is essential that no light reach the optical nerves in your eyes," he said. "Otherwise, you may find yourselves irreparably blind."

"What the heck are we getting into?" Monk gulped.

"Whatcha say?" demanded a harsh voice at Monk's back.

"I said you oughta brought a velocipede," Monk growled.

"Yeah?" snarled the other.

"Sure," Monk confided. "Then you wouldn't have to ride my heels like you been doin'!"

"That is the spirit," said the voice. "Keep up your nerve. There is no danger."

A moment afterward, they were precipitated into another chemical tank. This one was the most unpleasant of all. Clambering out, Monk felt strange. All of his body seemed filled with unholy fire.

A black room was next. It was long and narrow, and along one side of it was what felt like a bench.

The commanding voice said, "You will each stretch full length on the conveyor and lie perfectly quiet."

The conveyor proved to be the bench-like affair, and Monk and Doc reclined there with the others. The frightful flame in their bodies seemed to leap and surge and consume them, leaving only a sluggish hull from which the interior had been burned, with even their brains enveloped. Monk realized this meant they were approaching complete unconsciousness.

Unexpectedly, the conveyor began to move.

WHAT followed was not so bad, largely because they were virtually insensible. As they passed through a chamber which was filled with an intense blue haze, coldness followed the bodily fire. Next there was a long tube filled with a play of weirdly colored sparks which came in crashing discharges— the sound which Doc and Monk had heard on first entering the weird place.

Another liquid bath followed, after which there was a tube filled with an even more blue haze, and frightful pain. At that point, something happened to their eyes, and they could see no more. Monk was filled with an apprehension that he was permanently blinded, and he endeavored mightily to sit up, to move, to do something, anything—but he could not stir.

He heard a voice. It was Telegraph Edmunds, the homely chemist decided.

"Some one had better go and get those fellows Ham and Marikan," Telegraph was saying. "We will take care of them next."

Then Monk lost all comprehension of what went on around him.

Chapter 14

SPOOK WAR

HAM, lying where he had been held by the invisible men for almost an hour, heard heavy footsteps approaching from the direction of the fur farm, saw the marsh grass bending, and observed deep prints appear in the soft earth. He knew the invisible men had come for himself and Marikan.

Marikan also saw.

"A crazy man, this will make me!" he wailed.

"Pipe down!" said an invisible man roughly, and Ham and Marikan were lifted and borne toward the fur farm.

Ham, being the lighter, was carried much the faster, and was soon inside the house. He was handed down into the first enameled room. This was large. At first, he thought only Telegraph Edmunds was present, then it dawned on him that the room was literally crowded with invisible men.

A door opened and a stretcher seemed to float in, was lowered to the floor and turned over, so that its burden was deposited on the floor.

"How many more?" Telegraph Edmunds asked.

"Two," replied a voice from an invisible source. "Then we will be ready for you to go through."

"All right," said Telegraph. I'll handle this other first."

He went out, was gone a few moments, and came back with the invisible men bearing Marikan. The latter seemed to be in the last stages of terror.

Telegraph looked about the room, posing before the invisible audience he knew was watching him, and winked elaborately.

"The invisible processing will work on dead as well as live bodies," he said. "We will shoot this man Marikan, and Ham, then put them through and dump their bodies in the creek. Being invisible, the corpses will never be found."

Marikan wailed, "No, no! Not to me, don't do it! Let me join you! I can help! I am good chiropractor, and if you a pain in the back get, maybe I can——"

"It's a pain in the neck, you are!" Telegraph snorted. "Tie him, men."

Ropes came snaking out of a pile in the corner and

seemed to wrap themselves about Marikan, after which Telegraph seized him, drew a revolver, spun the cylinder, and dragged Marikan into the passage which led to the first processing room.

There was a moment of silence. Marikan began screaming, blubbering pleas for mercy. A shot made an ear-splitting bang. After that there was silence, until the pounding of Telegraph's feet broke it as he came back.

"Now the other one," he said.

It seemed that the shot sound still rang in the cavern.

At least, it seemed that the shot echoes still seeped about, as far as Monk was concerned. The homely chemist was vaguely aware that he was experiencing something he had never expected to feel again: consciousness. The crash of the shot seemed to have revived him. He sat up and looked around.

He was in the white-enameled room, and he saw Telegraph Edmunds with the revolver in his hand still curling a trace of smoke, and Ham, who was being held, it seemed, by unseen hands.

Monk sat up, tried to stand, and, much to his surprise, succeeded. But he was not erect for long. A spasm of dizziness seized him, got the best of him and he fell heavily.

Without looking around, Telegraph Edmunds said, "Do not try to move around too much when you first revive. It won't hurt you, but you'll be pretty dizzy."

That surprised Monk vastly. He brought his hands up to his head. Then he discovered something, something so uncanny that he distinctly felt his eyes squeeze out of their sockets and a parade of cold chills travel his spine. He shook his arms to be sure. He even touched his own nose.

"Blazes!" he gurgled aloud. "I just ain't!"

Monk had found himself to be invisible.

He got up again, and this time managed to stand. He walked, promptly stumbled over a prone figure, and elicited a groan. The stretcher came in again and deposited another invisible man.

Telegraph Edmunds was examining his revolver.

"This bird Ham will be next," he said.

That wrenched Monk out of the horrified trance which his personal fate had woven. He moved toward Ham, dodging away from Telegraph Edmunds and trying to keep behind him, until he realized that he could not be seen. Then he advanced boldly and crouched beside Ham, intending to whisper in the dapper lawyer's ear.

He never succeeded. A sudden, awful clutch laid hold of him. He was yanked upright, and felt fingers racing along the back of his neck. That told him who his invisible assailant was.

"Doc!" he squawked.

"Monk!" came a voice out of thin air—the bronze man's voice. "Break for it! I'll handle Ham!"

Telegraph Edmunds, slack-jawed with astonishment, roared, "What in blue hades is going on here?"

He got his answer when there was a sudden, terrific scuffle around Ham. Then Ham was lifted and borne with astonishing speed toward the door.

TELEGRAPH EDMUNDS began to yell orders at the top of his voice. He lifted his revolver.

But Monk was ready for that. He had lunged to Telegraph's side, and as the gun came up, he struck the man's arm a terrific blow. Telegraph not only howled and dropped his weapon, but fell down as well.

Monk ran for the steps. He joined Doc Savage at the top, inside the room of the fur-farm house.

Escape, it developed, was far from complete, since other invisible men were about outside. They came into the room so silently that they were not heard, and seized upon Ham.

The fight was short. The attackers had not reckoned upon the presence of Doc Savage and Monk, both invisible. Ham, freed, stumbled for the door.

"Run for it!" Doc Savage told him. "Monk and I will follow you. That way, we will not get lost from each other."

They followed that system, sprinting down the road at full speed until they heard a shout behind them, then ducking off into the marsh grass. They made straight for the nearest road, a distance of fully two miles, and traveled it as swiftly as possible.

A car came spinning along. Monk stood in the center of the road and cartwheeled his arms, only to realize at the last instant that he could not be seen. A wild leap got him clear.

"Blazes!" he complained aloud. "This being invisible is going to have its drawbacks!"

Ham squinted at the sound of the homely chemist's voice.

"You there, Monk?" he demanded.

"Sure," Monk grunted.

Ham smiled at the apparently empty space from which the childlike voice came.

"I must say that you look better than I ever expected you to look," he advised.

"Yeah?" Monk growled. "Well, there's another car coming."

Ham hailed that machine by lying prone in the road. The motorist, driving a ramshackle touring car, stopped and with great solicitude helped Ham who was pretending unconsciousness, into the car.

When the fellow drove off, Monk and Doc Savage were also in the rear seat.

Ham regained consciousness conveniently at the first filling station, and contrived to alight.

Doc Savage went into the filling station, lifted the telephone receiver and called the nearest State police station.

"You will find the headquarters of the invisible men on the fur farm owned by Angus Angelo Marikan," Doc announced, and gave the location of the skunk-raising establishment.

He could tell by the burst of excitement that there would be immediate and decisive action.

"Take bloodhounds to trail the invisible men," Doc advised.

"Who are you?" he was asked.

Doc hung up.

Turning, he saw the filling station attendant in the door. The man was starkly white and looked as if he were in the throes of a great terror. His throat muscles convulsed. His hands trembled. He must have heard the voice and seen the telephone receiver jump back on the hook, apparently by its own accord.

The man stumbled to a chair and sat down. He must have thought himself demented, for a moment, then he probably remembered the invisible men incidents in New York City.

"They're here!" he squawled. He dashed out through the door and ran at full speed down the road, not looking back.

Doc Savage went outside. Ham had gotten rid of the motorist who had picked him up, and was standing beside a gasoline pump. He heard Doc's footsteps, and knew the bronze man was near.

"How were you made invisible?" he demanded.

"I secured only a hazy idea of the process," Doc Savage explained. "It has something to do with altering the electronic composition of the body, securing an atomic motific status which results in complete diaphaneity."

"That," said Ham, "does not mean a lot to me."

"Nor a great deal more to me," the bronze man—he was possessed of neither form nor hue now, as far as appearances went—admitted. "The process was extremely involved. Monk and I lost consciousness before we were very far along. I do not know what happened after we were senseless."

Monk spoke up, causing Ham to start violently.

"We'll solve the mystery when the raiders clean the gang out of that skunk farm and we can examine the apparatus," he said.

Ham nodded. "Poor old Marikan. He was the goat all of the way through. They used him as a dummy owner of the farm, without his knowledge. Then they killed him."

Doc Savage started to comment, but withheld the words to listen to the wail of distant sirens. A speck appeared far down the road, grew larger, and became a careening State police car. Another followed, and another. In the last, there was a pack of bloodhounds. The noisy parade made for the fur farm.

At Doc's suggestion, Ham departed in the direction of New York City, with the understanding that he was to await Doc's appearance in the skyscraper headquarters.

Doc and Monk followed the New Jersey State troopers.

The troopers did their work efficiently. They deployed, circled the farm, and advanced. They scattered the bloodhounds so that an attack on any part of the line would be scented.

When they were still some distance from the farm buildings, the earth jumped, shook itself and emitted a great rumble. A cloud of débris jumped up at the fur farm simultaneously. That was the first of a series of nearly a dozen explosions.

The troopers broke into a run. Two were injured slightly when there was another underground blast, and they backed off to await quiet. Reassured, they went forward. Their first inspection showed that little of value would be found. The blast had been terrific, and whatever delicate machinery had been underground was now destroyed.

Moreover, there was no sign of the invisible men. The bloodhounds were put to work. The animals did much sniffing, and followed many trails to the edge of the creek. The troopers deployed, searched, and thereby discovered that there had been at least two boats concealed some distance down the stream. These were gone now, and the invisible men with them.

Doc Savage and Monk—they kept track of each other by observation and by exchanging a word now and then—watched the fiasco from a distance.

"Blast it!" Monk complained. "Now we *are* up in the air. We haven't got another clue to go on!"

He fell silent, watching a stirring in the grass near by, thinking at first that it was a rabbit or other small animal. Then the homely chemist emitted a glad howl.

"Habeas Corpus!" he exploded.

The shote had come through the marsh grass, apparently having scented Monk or heard his voice. He broke into a gallop, approaching.

"Habeas!" Monk chuckled, and advanced.

Habeas stopped. His ears stood out straight, and the coarse hairs on his nape hackled. He emitted a skeptical grunt or two.

"It's tough, hog, but you've now got a spook for an owner," Monk said.

Habeas made his ears stiffer. He grunted again, explosively. Then he spun and fled, taking tremendous leaps as if to take advantage of the gliding power inherent in his enormous ears.

"Hey, blast it," Monk called. "It ain't as bad as that!"

The homely chemist set out in pursuit, but did not overhaul Habeas until the latter was held up in swimming a stretch of water which Monk could wade. Monk grasped his porker by one flapping ear and carried him, a grunting, suspicious and disgusted shote, toward the road.

HALF an hour later, a truck driver was surprised to discover a pig with enormous ears riding in the rear of his vehicle. The truck was loaded with seed potatoes, and the driver threw one at the pig.

His hair stood on end when a child-like voice out of thin air advised him, "Hey, guy! That ain't no way to act!"

The driver was so doubtful of his own mental balance that he alighted at the first roadside lunch stand and took on the stimulation of hot coffee. When he went out, the pig was gone.

A taxi driver found the pig in the rear of his machine next, and later, a motorist who had passed through the Holland Tunnel under the Hudson River also found the porker. The pig fled when a capture was attempted.

None of these individuals suspected that two men, spectral in that they were entirely invisible, were accompanying the pig. They did note that the pig seemed frightened and entirely disgusted with the course events were taking.

In getting uptown with the porker, Doc Savage and Monk experienced some difficulty, but finally managed by filching more rides in taxicabs and other vehicles. There was a fruit stand near where they finally alighted, close to the skyscraper which housed Doc Savage's headquarters.

"I'm gonna try something," Monk decided.

Several persons stared at the sound of the voice. The proprietor of the fruit stand gaped as an apple left its rack and began to separate into good-sized bites, to the accompaniment of a juicy crunching.

Monk, mouth full of apple, demanded, "Do you see the blame thing after it's in my mouth, Doc?"

"Yes," Doc advised him. "And you better get it out, or the crowd will be chasing that piece of apple all over town."

Monk hastily spat the apple out.

Chapter 15

THE LIFE OF A GHOST

EXCITEMENT was as real as a cloud over the skyscraper which housed Doc Savage's headquarters. All of the doors and the lower-floor windows had been closed by stout wire screens. Entrance and exit from the lobby was being accomplished by a revolving affair of wire netting which resembled a revolving door, the partitions only large enough to pass one figure at a time.

Policemen were everywhere, heavily armed. They felt carefully in the rotating door affair to make sure no invisible persons were getting inside.

"Blazes!" Monk breathed. "What's this mean?"

They planted Habeas Corpus under a parked car where he would not attract attention, and loitered about, listening, stepping out of the path of such pedestrians as came past. It was not long before they heard an enlightening conversation between two policemen.

"You say they got one of Doc Savage's men in the can?" the first cop asked.

"The one called Ham," agreed the second officer. "He showed up here and they nabbed him and took him down to Centre Street."

Doc Savage and Monk stood aside as several elderly, bespectacled and scholarly-looking gentlemen got out of a limousine and were passed into the skyscraper by the officers.

"Who are the great brains?" one of the cops asked when the party was inside.

"Scientists," replied the other. "They've found a lot of queer instruments and apparatus in Doc Savage's laboratory, and they're going over it to see if it isn't stuff he has used to make himself and his gang invisible."

Doc and Monk withdrew with that, and held a consultation.

"The stupes!" Monk grumbled. "The only apparatus in the laboratory is stuff that has been there some time, and is probably too advanced for the average expert to understand. It has nothing to do with invisible men."

"Certainly not," Doc agreed; then added, "We had better get Ham out of jail."

They caught an elevated train down to Centre Street, the journey being made interesting by the efforts of train attendants to put the pig, Habeas Corpus, off the train. Twice these gentlemen succeeded, and Monk and Doc merely caught following trains.

They paused at a newsstand to read the latest headlines:

INVISIBLE MAN CHIEF IDENTIFIED!

HE IS DOC SAVAGE

They went on without reading more.

"That's a danged lie," Monk complained.

"Some one is jumping at conclusions," Doc agreed.

In order not to lose each other they linked hands when nearing street corners, and, at other times, they merely kept watch of the pig, Habeas Corpus. The porker was proving convenient as a visible link by which they could keep track of each other.

It was near the noon hour and they passed a group of chattering office girls, out for lunch.

"*Whew!*" Monk exploded, when the femininity was behind. "Is my face red!"

"Yes?" Doc prompted.

"Do you realize," Monk asked, "that we're walking down the street without a thing on?"

EVIDENCE that the invisible man scare had settled heavily upon the city could be seen frequently. Many jewelry establishments were closed, and others were fitted with little revolving doors of screened construction. Banks were also equipped with the rotating doors, and guards were feeling carefully to see that only visible individuals were admitted to the money houses.

Newsboys were already hoarse from howling headlines, and

were vending their wares by waving them wildly. There was little need for salesmanship anyway, since each batch of extra papers was absorbed almost as soon as it was unloaded from the fast delivery trucks.

Habeas Corpus stopped beside a newsstand, and Doc Savage knew Monk must have paused to read more headlines. When the pig went on, Doc also trailed, and a moment later Monk found the bronze man.

"This is a fine mess!" the homely chemist growled. "The newspapers say there's already been more than fifty robberies, all of them big ones. Telegraph Edmunds and his invisible men are cleaning up."

"We will try to get some line on them after we free Ham," Doc replied.

They had some little difficulty in locating Ham, but eventually found him confined in what was supposed to be an escapeproof portion of the jail. In freeing Ham, they found it necessary to overpower two guards.

Doc Savage did this by exerting a pressure against spinal nerve centers, a harmless process entailing no great pain, which brought an unconsciousness that would wear off shortly. Doc himself unlocked Ham's cell.

Ham backed away, put up his fists and refused to come out until Doc spoke to him.

"Oh!" Ham gulped. "I was afraid it was some of Telegraph's gang."

Once clear of the station, they took a taxicab, Ham entering the vehicle and giving directions to the driver. They left the machine uptown, mingled with the crowd, then caught another cab, left it after a time, and walked to the exclusive establishment where Ham, whose legal career had been so honorable before he joined Doc Savage, maintained bachelor lodgings.

The elevator operator had no idea that his car carried aloft any one other than Ham and Habeas. The hallway on Ham's floor was empty. They walked toward his apartment.

A peculiar thing had happened to the demeanor of Habeas Corpus. In the past, the pig had never been known to have anything to do with Ham. Now he trailed along at Ham's heels, and seemed happy enough to do it. He only grunted disgustedly and sidled away violently when the invisible Monk tried to pick him up.

"I thought better of you, Habeas," Monk grunted.

They entered Ham's apartment and the dapper lawyer went at once to a case and lifted out a sword cane, an exact duplicate of the one which he had carried earlier and which had vanished somewhere in the previous excitement. Ham kept an assortment of the canes. He flourished the weapon.

"Now I feel better," he announced.

"Then maybe we can talk," suggested a high, querulous voice.

HAM started violently. The voice did not belong to Doc or Monk. He was sure of that. He promptly sidled into a corner and unsheathed his sword cane, prepared to put up a defense. There was an invisible man in the room!

"All right," Ham snapped grimly. "Just what is the next move?"

"Conversation, as I told you," said the squeaky voice of the invisible man.

Ham was an actor, and he showed by no glance that Doc and Monk were also in the room. Too, he had recognized the venerable voice.

"Old Bonepicker," he said.

"I believe people call me that," admitted the invisible man, who had apparently been waiting in the apartment.

"What do you want?" Ham asked.

"Doc Savage," said Old Bonepicker. "P. Treve Easeman and myself wish to talk to him."

"I have not seen Doc Savage for some time," Ham replied —truthfully.

The pig, Habeas, apparently baffled by the phenomena of so many invisible men, grunted loudly and scuttled under the most convenient chair.

Old Bonepicker began speaking rapidly, earnestly.

"Easeman and myself have been doing some wondering," he said. "It is strange that we were selected as the first victims to be made invisible, in the plot to extort money from us to make us visible again. This is especially inexplicable in view of the conduct of Easeman's daughter and that Russel Wray, if you get my meaning."

Ham frowned and fingered his sword cane, still keeping the blade alert.

"You mean that you think the girl and Wray may be working with Telegraph Edmunds and his gang?" he demanded.

"It is a thought which has occurred to us," said Old Bonepicker. "There are other suspicious circumstances of which you do not know. Suppose you come with me to Easeman, and we will discuss them."

"How is Easeman—recovering from the gun wounds he received in the plane?" Ham asked.

"Getting along nicely," Old Bonepicker answered. "Of

course, it was extremely difficult to dress a bullet wound that cannot be seen in a man who is also not apparent to the eye."

"I will go with you," Ham decided.

THREE quarters of an hour after the strange conference, Ham and Habeas Corpus, apparently alone, strode into an office suite in a skyscraper just outside the Wall Street sector of downtown New York City. There was a name on the office door:

EASEMAN ENTERPRISES, INC.
P. Treve Easeman, Pres.

"This is one of Easeman's offices," informed Old Bonepicker, who was clinging to Ham's arm.

Two pictures were prominent on the wall. One was of a distinguished, stoutly built man; the other was a slender, bony, hawk-faced fellow. Both were middle-aged men.

"The pictures are myself and Easeman," Old Bonepicker offered.

Ham surveyed the likenesses with interest, it being his first hint of what the two actually looked like.

"The slender one is you?" he asked.

"On the contrary, I am the stout one." Old Bonepicker's chuckle was a dry, ghostly rattle in the room. "My voice is somewhat deceptive, I am afraid."

"You and Easeman are friends?" Ham asked. "I mean—you were friends before this affair materialized?"

"We were," said Old Bonepicker. "We had business dealings."

Ham nodded. "Where is Easeman?"

"In the inner office."

Ham himself closed the door, and surreptitiously operated the lock, fixing it so that the door would not fasten. The lawyer wanted the way open for Doc Savage to enter, along with Monk, and overhear what was to be said.

Ham was guided into the inner office, a rich room fitted with a large desk, upholstered business chairs, filing cabinets and a leather divan.

"Easeman is on the divan," Old Bonepicker advised.

Ham looked at the divan and felt the short hairs on his nape stir, simply because there was nothing whatever on the divan but a dressing such as might have been over a wound. This lay a little above the leather of the divan. It was altogether ghostly.

Ham said, "Mr. Easeman, do you fell well enough to talk?"

There was a loud bang from the outer room, as if the door had slammed.

Ham half turned. Then he watched the divan. A large and businesslike revolver lifted from behind the couch and pointed at Ham.

"I am Easeman," a voice said from the divan. "You cannot see me, but you can see this gun. You will stand perfectly still."

"A trick," Ham exploded.

"Exactly!" said Old Bonepicker's voice. "I was surprised that you fell for it."

Ham snapped. "Why not? I wanted to find out what it was all about."

"You damned well know what it is all about," said P. Treve Easeman's voice.

There were more sounds from the outer office. Then the voice of the girl, Ada Easeman, called out.

"Come and help us!" she appealed. "I think Doc Savage and another man came inside after Ham. They are invisible!"

HAM stood perfectly still, for it seemed the best thing to do. Easeman heaved up from the divan. A shaking of the gun indicated the man was enfeebled.

"I will watch this lawyer," he said. "Bonepicker, you take care of Doc Savage."

Bonepicker backed away—crushing of the rug nap showed that—and entered the outer office. Ada Easeman was there, with a revolver. Russel Wray was also present, and likewise armed. They had their backs to the door. Their eyes were fixed on the apparently empty office.

"Where is Doc Savage and the other one?" Old Bonepicker asked.

"In here somewhere," the girl replied.

Wray now removed the key from the outer door. He and the girl separated, bent over and picked up corners of the rug. It was obvious that the room had been prepared beforehand for just such a procedure.

Old Bonepicker slammed the door at his own back, closing the office.

The rug covered most of the floor area. It was lifted and, like a huge net, brought forward. An instant later, it was evident an invisible man had been netted.

Wray yelled, hurled the rug over the unseen one, and sprang atop the squirming bulk.

A pained howl came out of the rug. No one who had ever

heard that voice would have trouble identifying it again.

"It's the one called Monk!" barked Old Bonepicker. "Get him!"

All three of them hurled upon Monk. In the terrific fight that followed, the invisible Monk tore the rug and nearly managed to escape.

Wray hammered madly with his gun. It struck something that sounded like wood. The struggles ceased.

"Hit him on the head!" Wray rapped triumphantly.

They got cords and proceeded to tie the unconscious Monk. Wray then secured a bottle of ink and poured it on the captive, thus making some of his outlines visible.

A search was pushed for Doc Savage. They lifted the rug in the inner office and advanced carefully, as if seining. The result was a blank.

"But he must have come in!" Old Bonepicker insisted querulously.

They searched again. They went over the office with infinite care, and even seined a small washroom which adjoined the inner sanctum. They lifted the washroom window and looked out, shaking their heads when they saw the sheer expanse of bricks outside.

Ham watched them in noncommittal silence. When they entered the washroom, he held his breath. He knew something they did not suspect. He had seen the washroom door open furtively and close with infinite silence, after which he thought he had heard the window open and close. Ham rather suspected that Doc Savage had departed by that route.

"What are you going to do with me?" Ham demanded.

RUSSEL WRAY came over and glared at the dapper lawyer. Wray's face was sullen, and his lip, which had been injured in the brawling the night before, had swollen, cocking his white mustache up.

The girl came over and stood beside Wray. She was still garbed in her emerald evening gown, but it was showing the effects of strenuous action. The wrinkled state of the frock seemed to detract no whit from her unquestionable beauty.

"Doc Savage is the chief of the invisible horde," Wray said.

Ham snorted. "You are wasting your time trying to kid me. You are mixed up in it yourself! That came out at Old Bonepicker's house."

"If you mean what the liar, Marikan, said, you are mistaken!" the girl snapped. "We did not handcuff him."

"Marikan is dead," Ham said.

Wray sniffed unbelievingly. "Who killed him?"

"Telegraph Edmunds," Ham advised. "No doubt you know that very well."

The girl and Wray exchanged glances.

"He is lying, of course," the girl said. "Doc Savage is a scientific wizard, and no doubt discovered how to make men invisible and is now trying to cash in on it."

The tones of P. Treve Easeman interrupted. "Well, question this fellow and find out where Doc Savage has his machine for making men invisible."

"Don't think we won't do that!" Wray said grimly.

They grasped Ham and smashed him down on the leather divan and tied him securely, then expended several minutes in trying to catch the pig, Habeas. The porker, however, proved so agile that they were forced to permit him to remain at large.

Old Bonepicker asked, "What will we do with this lawyer fellow if he will not talk?"

"The same thing that we will do with him in any event," said P. Treve Easeman—"turn him over to the police."

Ham frowned. Suddenly he lifted his voice to its greatest volume, which was surprising, for he had trained himself to make his natural voice carry to the limits of the largest courtrooms.

"Doc!" he shouted. "They're going to turn me over to the police when they are done! I believe they are honestly trying to find the chief of the invisible men!"

Chapter 16

THE SPOOK DETECTOR

Doc Savage heard the shout emitted by Ham, and understood the words, a fact which influenced his future procedure to a marked degree.

The outside of the skyscraper was not as insurmountable as it had appeared to the girl and Wray. One skilled in the art of the so-called "human fly," and possessed of nerve and unnaturally strong fingers, can climb a surface which would baffle the layman. It is the combination of height and the fear of falling which defeats them, rather than the lack of finger purchases.

The bronze man was near a window to which he had

gone from time to time to rest. Since he was invisible, it was not necessary for him to worry about being seen. He clambered to the window now. The office beyond was full of stenographers and clerks at work.

Doc Savage placed a palm against the pane and managed to shake the window so that it made considerable noise. This disgusted a clerk and the fellow came over, lifted the window in an endeavor to see what was wrong, and Doc Savage slipped inside.

It was impossible to avoid brushing against the clerk, and this startled the latter, although not to the point that he realized what had happened.

An elevator operator answered what he must have concluded was a fake call; and on the twelfth floor, where there was another ring, a woman got on with a dog, and the canine behaved very strangely going down, howling and barking, much to the mystification of its owner.

Doc Savage experimented with the dog, bending over and touching it, and it was evident that the animal knew of his presence only because of the sense of smell, and was unable to see him.

Out on the street, the bronze man found the sidewalks completely filled with noontime crowds. So thick was the throng that he had difficulty avoiding persons. This problem he solved by getting behind a uniformed policeman who seemed bent for some definite destination. There was a cleared space for walking behind the cop, due to the instinct which makes people instinctively step wide of a policeman.

Doc caused an uproar in the subway station, more from absentmindedness than anything else. From force of habit, in leaving the station uptown, he passed out through one of the turnstiles. The man in the ticket booth saw the stile turn, and was quickwitted enough to realize the truth. He emitted a series of howls which filled the station with uniformed officers, but not before Doc Savage was safely on his way.

On the street, he discovered it highly dangerous to jaywalk, and but by the grace of an agile leap did he escape the wheels of a speeding motorist. He landed in a puddle of gutter water, and in walking on, left a procession of wet footprints. These were seen by a woman who promptly fainted, and a bedlam of yelling went up.

Doc raced to the nearest newsstand and wiped his feet on newspapers while the proprietor stood still and yelled his terror. After that, no tracks were deposited.

Doc then clung to an open trolley car, stepped from there to a taxicab fender without touching the ground, and alighted when the taxi turned onto another street, thus thwarting any endeavor to use bloodhounds to trail him.

He finally reached the skyscraper which housed his headquarters.

THE guards and netting turnstiles were still in place before the doors, and only persons who could prove occupancy of the building, and those with urgent business, were being admitted. Doc Savage did not attempt to wrangle his way inside.

He sought a marine store near by which sold yacht supplies, and since attempting to purchase an article would only have caused great excitement, he appropriated a small grapple and a hank of stout line, which he would pay for later. He got these out through the rear door without any one noticing that they were seemingly floating in thin air.

Alleyways, side doors, and even the ruse of holding the package so close to the side of a pedestrian that it would seem he was carrying it, got Doc into a department store building across the street from the skyscraper which held his headquarters. He worked to the roof of this.

There were many offices unoccupied for the day in the skyscraper across the street, due to the difficulty in gaining admission and the quite natural disinclination of persons to put themselves in proximity with the invisible menace.

Doc selected a window which was open, waited until he was sure the office behind it was not occupied, and hurled the grapple, to one end of which the line had been made fast.

It was not a throw that required supernatural ability, but it did take nice calculating, and Doc missed the first time. The clang of the hook drew people to windows, although Doc got hook and rope back before they saw it. He waited until they went away, then tried again, and succeeded.

The hook caught on the sill inside. He tested with a yank that put far more strain than his weight on the rope. Then he made the other end of the line fast about a ventilator.

In swinging out over the street, Doc kept a tight grip on the rope, so that, should the grapple give, he would be ready to cling to the line and attempt to break his smashing swing against the other building. But the crossing was without such incident.

He entered the office, let himself out, and rode an elevator secretly to the eighty-sixth floor. The door of his office was barred with wire, and the corridor was filled with armed men. Doc withdrew to the floor below, where there was a secret door back of a fire cabinet which gave to a ladder leading up to the laboratory room.

A moment later, he was in the laboratory.

SOME six men were present in the laboratory. None of them were young, and they all had the appearance of men who had devoted their lives to learning. They were going over the apparatus in the laboratory, handling the contrivances delicately, congregating around the more advanced devices, attempting to ascertain their nature.

"One of the most remarkable collections of scientific apparatus in existence, no doubt," said the man, and waved an arm to include all of the great room. "You might say that here is concentrated the learning of man since the beginning of time. No wonder this man Savage is considered to be something of a mental marvel."

"I would give a good many years of my life for this laboratory," said another. "With it, marvels can be accomplished, true enough. Take, for instance, this device for light analysis of metals. In a few minutes, it can equal the work of hours by ordinary methods."

Doc Savage advanced. He had come to the laboratory to get a portable kit, property of the homely Monk, which was probably one of the most complete chemical analysis and compounding units of its size in existence. The bronze man took half a dozen steps, paused, and his eyes rested steadily on a glass shelf.

There was an ordinary electroscope on the shelf. Its leaves were standing apart.

Doc Savage retreated. The electroscope leaves came together slightly. He advanced. The leaves flew apart.

FOR a long time the invisible giant stood there, considering the electroscope phenomena. The device was affected, of course, by static electricity, and would behave variously in the presence of radioactive materials. Obviously, the bronze man's body, in its invisible state, was giving off an emanation, or perhaps was only impregnated with a static charge, which affected the electroscope.

Doc Savage tried various experiments, unnoticed by the scientists who were going over the equipment. He grounded his body. This seemed to have no effect on the reaction of the electroscope. When he had finished, he knew that he had at hand a detector which would indicate the presence of invisible men.

There was more than one electroscope in the laboratory, and Doc Savage gathered together a number of these, using cotton to pad them, and inserting them in a stout carton which he carried down into the secret entrance.

Due to the necessity of accomplishing his mission without being observed, he was delayed fully an hour.

The line by which he had crossed the street was thin and up high, and had escaped notice. Carrying the box of electroscopes and Monk's portable laboratory, which was contained in metal cases, Doc Savage was almost across the rope before he—the load, rather—was seen from the street below. A cop, unusually alert, was the discoverer. He cut loose instantly with his gun. With mad haste, Doc swung the remaining distance.

Nor did he tarry in the department store. Racing down from the roof, he ran to the elevators. The simple sight of the metal boxes and package floating into the elevator was enough to send all other occupants fleeing. Doc ran the cage down.

Police guards were already at the street doors. Doc sought the rear, found a window and managed to drop through without damaging his burden. There was a taxi stand at the corner, and one of the machines was unoccupied.

Doc placed his burden in the driverless cab, then entered a cigar store which had a telephone booth from which the cab could be watched. There was no one near the telephone. He dialed police headquarters.

"This is Doc Savage," he said. "Ordinary electroscopes can be used to detect the presence of the invisible men. Issue them to your policemen. Next to that, bloodhounds are your best bet."

He pressed the hook down on a storm of excited questions. Next, he looked up the number of P. Treve Easeman's downtown office in the directory, then dialed and got an answer. It was Old Bonepicker who replied.

"How are my assistants, Monk and Ham?" Doc asked.

Old Bonepicker swore.

"They haven't talked, and we are going to turn them over to the police!" he squeaked.

"Very well," Doc told him. "I merely wished to ascertain that they were safe."

Over the telephone, he heard Monk and Ham both yell out simultaneously in perfectly healthy voices, apparently by way of showing that they were not greatly damaged.

The wire went dead as Old Bonepicker hung up.

Chapter 17

SEIZURE

OLD BONEPICKER glared at the telephone angrily after he had cracked the receiver back in place.

"The nerve of that big fellow!" he gritted.

Attractive Ada Easeman, standing at Old Bonepicker's elbow, asked doubtfully, "Could it be that Doc Savage is not the head of this gang, after all?"

"Bosh!" Old Bonepicker snorted. "You're letting his looks sway you!"

For that, the young woman sniffed at the spot where Old Bonepicker, absolutely invisible, was standing.

"What are you going to do?" she asked.

"Call the police," said Old Bonepicker. "That's what we should have done long ago."

The telephone lifted from the desk in ghostly fashion as he picked it up, the receiver jumped from the hook, and he requested the number of police headquarters. He seemed to have a good knowledge of who was who in the department, for he called for the detective bureau chief of that district by name.

"We are holding two of Doc Savage's men in the office of P. Treve Easeman," he said, and gave the exact location of the office. "We also have some information that will help you. Better come at once."

"Are these two Doc Savage assistants invisible?" asked the detective.

"One of them is," said Old Bonepicker.

"Brother, we'll be right over!" the lawman roared, and slammed the telephone down on the desk.

The police detective upset his chair, such was his haste in arising. There were buttons on his desk for summoning subordinates. He pounded these.

"Two of Doc Savage's men being held!" he yelled.

Then he gave the address of Easeman's office.

The words were loud, calculated to carry to all of the policemen rushing into the room in answer to the buzzer summons.

A fractional moment later, a wadded chunk of paper near

the door changed position, as if it had been kicked. There was no one near. The rear stairway had not been dusted recently, and fresh tracks appeared mysteriously in the dust. That was all that indicated the movement of an invisible man—until the door of a parked sedan down the street came open.

"By hanging around the police department, I got a line on two of Doc Savage's men, if not on Doc Savage himself!" said the voice of Telegraph Edmunds. "The two are being held in Easeman's office. Get down there, quick!"

There was a driver in the seat of the car. His face was an unusual brown color, and a close scrutiny would have shown that it was not his face at all which showed, but a covering of very thin rubber, a hoodlike mask which could be drawn on and taken off. He wore goggles to disguise the empty holes that were his eyes, and his hands were encased in gloves. Only a more than casual inspection would have shown the truth.

The sedan hurtled away from the curbing. Voices indicated at least half a dozen men in the rear and possibly some clinging to the running boards, but those who looked into the car saw an apparently empty machine.

The party of invisible men got into the P. Treve Easeman office building without attracting attention, and filched rides on an elevator. On the cage, they had a mishap. It chanced that all other passengers alighted before the Easeman floor was reached.

"Twenty-eight," said Telegraph Edmunds, thinking to deceive the operator.

But the operator looked around, saw the empty cage and let out a screech, guessing instantly who his passengers were. The unlucky attendant was slugged, beaten into insensibility, and his car run on up.

TELEGRAPH EDMUNDS knocked boldly on the Easeman office door.

"Who is it?" asked Ada Easeman.

"Police!" boomed Telegraph.

Ada Easeman unlocked the door. Instantly, Telegraph's invisible companions hit it, battering it open. The girl cried out, but she might as well have saved her breath, for the unseen assailants flooded into the offices. In a moment they had found Old Bonepicker and Easeman, simply because they wielded guns, hoping to see a target, and the weapons marked their positions so that they could be seized.

Russel Wray was caught flat-footed and knocked down before he could resist effectively. The girl was also floored by main strength.

"Beautiful!" chuckled Telegraph Edmunds. "Beautiful! It could not have worked out better. Now we only have to get Doc Savage."

"Oh!" exclaimed Ada Easeman. "Then he is not working with you?"

Telegraph snorted. "He's working *on* us!"

No time was wasted. The prisoners, visible and invisible, were bound and gagged, and the purloined elevator was employed to carry them, not to the lobby, but to the basement level, from whence they were spirited, by great good luck and much caution, out into the sedan. They were forced to lie on the floor.

As the sedan pulled away, police cars came down the street, sirens screaming. There was an extremely large force of officers, the gathering of which probably accounted for the delay. They alighted, and jointed hands in a line across the front of the office building. Their superiors went up, to have their confidence shattered when they found their birds had been removed.

Half an hour later, the story was in the newspapers. In the newspapers also was the matter of the telephone call concerning the electroscopes which Doc Savage had made. One tabloid had sent a squad of reporters out with an electroscope, and the leaves of the thing flew apart when they neared the first bank, indicating an invisible man. The latter had escaped, however, but not until there had been quite an uproar.

The invisible man had no doubt been standing by, trying to figure out a way of getting into the bank. The bank promptly closed, announcing it would do no more business until the invisible man menace was squashed.

The newsboys, such of them as had not already howled themselves hoarse, ran about crying the new developments.

Doc Savage heard the shouting, and read the story over a fat man's shoulder. The bronze man did the reading by spurts, devoting most of his attention to the sedan bearing Telegraph Edmunds and his prisoners.

Doc had arrived at the Easeman office just in time to follow the raiders and their captives down to the sedan. Doc had ridden clinging to the tire carrier.

THE sedan was waiting before the entrance of a private garage in the uptown section of the city, a rather respectable residence district, and one of the invisible men had no doubt gone inside to open the door and admit the car.

Doc Savage waited. The street was quiet, although far from deserted, and traffic rolled slowly. On the nearest corner, three or four houses away, there was a subway station, the entrance newly constructed, but the entry was boarded over. This was evidently a part of the newly constructed subway system, not yet opened to the public.

The subway ventilating gratings were spaced along the sidewalk. Out of these came the moan of a train. Doc Savage, who knew the subterranean tracks were not carrying passenger trains as yet, decided it must be a work train.

The garage door opened, unlocked from the interior. Doc Savage sidled up alongside the sedan as it began to move. It was fortunate that he had gone immediately to the Easeman office.

The car passed into what seemed to be a very ordinary garage, stopped, and the driver got out. He removed the tight rubber facial mask, which was probably uncomfortable, and pulled off his chauffeur's coat. He discarded his hat. The result, a pair of shoes and trousers parading about, was uncanny to a point where even the invisible men themselves were affected.

"Be fish or fowl, guy!" a voice suggested. "Either get them pants and shoes off, or put on some more clothes. You give me the creeps!"

The chauffeur chuckled and kicked off his trousers. They had scarcely dropped to the garage floor when a clock inside the house struck twice.

"Two o'clock," said Telegraph Edmunds. "We had better get inside. Our men will be dropping in. They are all to be here by four."

"What's the idea?" some one asked.

"Conference," said Telegraph. "We've got to plan to-morrow's work. We'll operate in New York to-morrow, then shift to Chicago. That way, no extended preparations can be made for our capture. Two days in Chicago, and we will shift to another town."

A man announced, "Say, I'm hungry. How we gonna work this eating business?"

"Go ahead and eat, but lightly," Telegraph directed. "You'll find that the food is visible in your mouth and throat, but after it gets down, it almost instantly disappears. That is, unless you load up on grub. Do not eat much more than the equivalent of a sandwich."

"This being invisible is a funny business," another offered. "I'd like to know more about it."

"The big chief will show up at the four o'clock conference," Telegraph advised. "Ask him the questions. He's the guy who discovered the process."

"You sure he's actually got a machine that will make us visible again?" asked a skeptic.

"Positive," said Telegraph. "I've been through it. The thing works to perfection and only requires a few moments."

"That's swell," said the other. "I don't fancy this life of a spook any too much. I don't think my girl friend would like it."

"You keep away from the girl friend," snapped Telegraph.

"Don't worry," snorted the other, "she wouldn't stick around me like I am now."

The prisoners were being hauled out of the sedan.

"What'll we do with these?" an invisible man asked.

"Hold them until the chief gets here at four," directed Telegraph Edmunds.

A MAN asked, "What about the swag we've annexed?"

"That is being concealed at various places, and the chief is keeping a record on his person," Telegraph explained. "We will divide it up later."

The captives were carried into a room, bare of furniture and dusty. They were deposited roughly on the floor and their bindings examined.

Telegraph Edmunds called four names and the owners answered.

"You four watch the prisoners," Telegraph directed. "I'll station others about. We don't want them getting away."

"Listen," a man interrupted. "What about the bags for carrying the loot? I didn't have any to-day, and a cop damned near got me by shooting at a necklace I had snatched off an old dame."

"In the next room," Telegraph stated, "Come on and I will show them to you."

The showing process proved to be one of feeling rather. The invisible men went to a corner and touched piles of rough fabric which felt not unlike chain mail, and which was absolutely invisible to the naked eye.

"Seems to be metal," some one grunted.

"It is metal," Telegraph answered. "I know that much about it. Seems that the boss tried lots of different things, but decided on this alloy because it was lighter and besides, could be made invisible easier. It's just a cloth woven out of flexible wires."

They left the pile after a time and went into another room, where they spread themselves on chairs, quarreling mildly when a man would chance to select a chair in which another had already deposited himself.

However, some fifteen minutes later, a man did decide to go to the pile of invisible loot containers and get one, stating his purpose was to handle the thing to get its feel, so that he could manipulate the thing more readily.

"Get so I can find the mouth of the bag easy," he said.

He was not an unusually discerning individual, hence his sense of touch did not inform him that the pile of bags was somewhat smaller than it had been a few minutes earlier.

Chapter 18

UNMAKER OF SPOOKS

THERE was much wonder on the part of the city when the depredations of the invisible legion ceased shortly before four o'clock that afternoon, although it did not dawn immediately—except to the police department, who had been swamped by calls all day—that the manipulations of the spook horde had stopped. The policemen could not understand it, and did little but snatch time for hurried sandwiches.

In assembling at the uptown house where Monk, Ham and the other prisoners had been taken, the invisible men used more than average caution, for not once was their presence detected.

Nearly thirty of them gathered. It was not a large number, considering the furor they had raised, but they were not ordinary criminals. They were clever, the pick of Telegraph Edmunds's large acquaintance of confidence men, swindlers and other crooks of more than average ability. Any one could have donned suitable attire and mingled with the best society. There was not a mug among them.

They were a happy crew, but they kept their spirits down until they were inside the house, and even then, they did not permit their laughter to become too boisterous.

As one put it: "We've got the world by the tail, as long as we can keep from getting stepped on."

A few seconds after four o'clock, there was something of a commotion as an invisible man of more importance than the others arrived.

"The big chief, the man with brains enough to work this all out," Telegraph Edmunds announced.

The newcomer voiced no word.

"Do you want to outline future plans, chief?" Telegraph asked.

Something was evidently whispered in Telegraph's ear by the leader, something none of the others heard, for Telegraph cleared his throat and began to speak rapidly.

"Our operations so far have been highly profitable," he declared. "We have gathered, at a conservative estimate, some twenty millions of dollars in the course of the day. The newspapers are claiming that it is a great deal more, but it is actually around that sum, which, however, may shrink somewhat before we turn it into hard cash."

Telegraph was somewhat of a politician and knew how to keep his men happy, as well as encourage them to future efforts, for he now launched into a brief review of the more profitable crimes of the day, handing out praise to the participants. The meeting was developing into a regular conference.

Voices were kept low. The house was gloomy, and seemingly unoccupied, the doors being closed; the lookouts—one at each door—did not stir about, or even peer out into the street.

Perhaps that was a mistake. They would hardly have seen anything. But they might have heard some slight, although interesting sounds.

Doc Savage, who had been away from the house until slightly after four o'clock, was back again.

THE bronze man had purloined a delivery truck—hardly theft, because the vehicle belonged to a bakery concern in which he had a large interest. He had equipped himself with trousers, a ragged topcoat and a hat, and had walked boldly into a drug store and gotten grease paint from the section devoted to the sale of theatrical supplies. The grease paint had outlined his features with passable distinctness.

He had experienced more difficulty in getting what the truck held—coils of heavy insulated copper cable. There was an alley near by, and he parked the truck in this. No great labor was entailed in hoisting the insulated cable to the roof.

Doc Savage worked swiftly. He located an electric power line and hooked on to it with his cables, which were in turn connected to high-frequency spark coils. The latter, the bronze man had carried from an electrical supply house on lower Broadway.

From the coils, the copper cables were conducted to doors and windows of the house. There, the bronze man operated more painstakingly, employing a material which was as invisible as he himself, for he had removed clothing and grease paint.

When he had finished, he had strung over the doors and windows strands of the invisible metal fabric from which the loot bags had been woven. He went over all connections, making sure the insulated cables were connected to the invisible metal strands in the proper manner.

He hurried to a telephone in a drug store and called the same policeman to whom he had earlier given the information regarding the effectiveness of the electroscopes. He imparted the address of the house in which Telegraph Edmunds and the invisible legion were gathered.

"All of the invisible men are there," he advised. "Do not try to raid the place. Block the adjacent streets and rooftops with woven-wire fencing. Allow no loopholes whatever. Station men with spray guns, filled with ink or paint. Assemble your dogs. Have tear gas and laughing gas. In short, take every possible precaution."

The police official was silent for a time.

"This is not a gag?" he asked. "You know, your finger prints have been found on the scene of crime after crime which these invisible men have committed."

Doc Savage hurriedly explained about the finger tip impressions taken while he was unconscious.

"All right," said the officer.

"How many men can you assemble?" Doc asked.

"Five thousand," said the other.

"Not enough," Doc told him. "Call on the Brooklyn navy yard and the local army posts for reënforcements. If this attempt to corner the invisible men fails, there will probably never be another chance."

The official debated again. "I will have plenty of men."

Doc Savage hung up, went to a fire escape which he had lowered in the alley, and climbed to the roof. He walked through a cluster of pigeons; they obviously did not see him, for they did not fly.

There was a roof hatch, closed but not fastened. Doc Savage opened it.

A guard below heard the opening and growled, "What the hell?"

"Careful!" Doc hissed. "I think Doc Savage is around here somewhere."

"Yeah?" rasped the other. "Where?"

Doc had located the invisible man by his voice. He struck once, then again, then lunged with open arms and grasped the unconscious man before he could fall.

Doc descended stairs.

TELEGRAPH EDMUNDS had finished the preliminaries of his talk, and had neared the end of the plan to raid Chicago.

"Are there any questions?" he asked.

"What about the prisoners?" some one demanded.

"We might as well dispose of them," Telegraph said. "And that reminds me: There's something I want to ask Old Bonepicker."

The captives were now ordered hauled into the room, and Telegraph Edmunds found Old Bonepicker by the simple expedient of kicking each of the invisible prisoners and listening to them groan. He leaned over Old Bonepicker.

"Remember that fight at the airport, when I split my gang and part of them took off in the plane?" he snapped. "The plane got in the air, and something happened to it. An invisible man came down in a parachute. That was you, wasn't it? You caused that plane to crash and kill my men?"

Old Bonepicker made a snarling sound.

"They tried to kill me after they found me!" he grated. "Could I help it if the pilot, the only flier aboard, got knocked out in the scrap, and I dived overboard with the only parachute?"

"So that's the way it was," Telegraph grunted. "You're going to pay for that!"

If he expected a response from Old Bonepicker, he was disappointed. The elderly financier returned only silence.

"Aw, blazes!" somebody said. "Let's get it over with."

A man in the back of the room spoke up.

"One thing we ain't discussed," he said dryly. "And that's how we're gonna make ourselves visible again. Boy, that's an important point as far as I'm concerned."

"You said it," declared another. "If we have to stay invisible, a fine chance we've got to enjoy the proceeds of this little scheme. I'm beginning to get a first-class idea of why nobody ever heard of a cheerful ghost."

Telegraph Edmunds laughed.

"Would you feel any better," he demanded, "if you saw the apparatus which will make you visible again?"

"I sure would!" the man said.

"The door to the right," Telegraph directed. "Walk down the steps you will find, and open the door at the bottom."

The command was complied with, the amount of scuffling, jostling and growled comments indicating that most of the invisible men were going to see the device. They descended to a large basement room.

In the center of the room stood a complicated affair consisting, at a first glance, of high-voltage transformers, many coils, a long cylinder, and numerous electrical valves of the type used to generate Röntgen and other rays.

Telegraph Edmunds advanced.

"It is simple," he said. "All of the operations are synchronized. You simply throw the switch and put yourself in that cylinder and stay there until you are visible again." Telegraph raised his voice slightly. "Isn't that right, chief? You made the jigger."

A voice replied, "That is right. And now, the prisoners should be finished."

They went back. The first man in the room where the captives should have been emitted a violent yell.

There was no trace of the prisoners, all of whom had been tightly bound and gagged.

TELEGRAPH EDMUNDS, at a hissed suggestion from the mysterious chief of the raiders, dashed forward, shouting commands to the door guards. He had not taken many steps when there cracked out the sound of a loud blow. Telegraph fell heavily. He was not out, however.

"Watch it!" he bellowed.

The invisible men spread out. One cried out as he was slugged, and flailed about. He hit some one, friend or foe he knew not, and was struck back in return. Twenty seconds of that saw the room in an uproar.

Doc Savage circled warily, lashing out with his fists. He knew Monk and Old Bonepicker were somewhere in the room. Doc had freed them while the visibility device was being inspected. P. Treve Easeman, the girl and Russel Wray were in a stout closet, the door of which they had secured on the inside, if they had followed instructions.

A chair lifted from the floor, swung and cracked down on an invisible head. The rungs splintered. Monk bawled out wrathfully as some one hit him a blow.

Then an invisible man came charging from the direction of the door.

"The place is surrounded!" he squalled. "Cops! Soldiers! Sailors! A million of 'em! They've got woven wire up in the streets and on the buildings!"

The fighting in the room stopped as if by magic, ample proof that the invisible legion had been mauling each other.

"They're wise to this place!" Telegraph Edmunds yelled. "We'd better blow!"

A man wailed, "If they've got the place surrounded, how are we gonna get out?"

"Easy," said Telegraph. "We took care of that."

Barking orders, Telegraph Edmunds now backed down the

stairs to the room which held the visibility apparatus. There was a door across the chamber, and he opened it. A sloping tunnel was disclosed.

"Go down," he directed.

One of the invisible men barked, "Can't we take that jigger along?"

"What jigger?"

"The contraption to make us visible again."

"Not a chance," Telegraph advised.

"But can another one be made?" the man wanted to know.

"Of course," Telegraph retorted. "Just like we'll make another machine to cause men to become invisible, when we get around to it. Isn't that right?"

"Correct," said the voice of the leader. "Now, waste no more time. I will remain here until the last. Then, before I leave, I will smash this visibility device, in order that it may not fall into the hands of this Doc Savage."

The men began scrambling into the tunnel, feeling with their hands to keep from trampling on each other. Telegraph Edmunds waited until the last.

"That's all, chief," he informed.

"Go yourself," directed the leader. "I will follow."

Telegraph Edmunds grunted noisily as he wedged his plump bulk into the rather narrow tunnel.

A moment later, a large pipe wrench lifted from a bench which held tools in the corner. It floated through the air toward the delicate mechanism in the center of the floor, then lifted as if to strike. But it never fell.

There was a stifled gasp, then a blow, and the wrench fell to the floor.

"Glory be!" Monk snorted. "Doc, I figured you were waiting for him to do something to show where he was."

THE bronze man said rapidly, "I will follow them alone. They will expect their chief, and if they challenge me, I will try to imitate his voice."

"Swell," Monk replied. "And I'm gonna fix this baby so that he'll sleep for a while."

There was a robust *whack*, as if a fist had collided soundly with a jaw, as Monk made sure their prisoner would remain unconscious.

Doc Savage entered the tunnel. He was forced to turn sidewise to pass his shoulders through, and this made progress somewhat difficult, since the floor sloped steeply. He became conscious of a faint rumbling sound. Then he realized the cause.

He came out in an arched cavern as wide as a city street

and which stretched away an infinite distance in either direction. It was the tunnel of the newly completed subway.

Telegraph Edmunds hailed Doc Savage sharply: "That you, chief?"

Doc assumed the voice he had heard.

"Let's get going," he said shortly.

"O. K.," said Telegraph. "I've started the boys out to the east."

Doc Savage got in the middle of the tracks and ran. Ahead, the tunnel sloped downward sharply, and the bronze man knew that the decline meant that it was leading under the river. Some three quarters of a mile ahead, the tunnel came up again, and there was a station exit by which the invisible men no doubt intended to depart.

Doc stopped abruptly. The roaring noise he had heard was growing louder. It was a train, a work train possibly, coming from behind.

"Careful!" he called suddenly. "There is not much room in the tunnel to let that train pass."

Telegraph Edmunds swore harshly, then grated, "We'll fix that!"

Stacked beside the tracks, and arrayed neatly between the supports between the two lines of rails, were numerous pieces of metal equipment—tools not yet hauled away by the subway contractor, Telegraph Edmunds howled orders, and these tools were seized and thrown upon the rails.

Doc Savage started to order a stop, but held the words back, realizing they would betray his presence.

"Run!" Telegraph howled, when he decided enough objects littered the track to guarantee derailing the train. "Get down the tunnel far enough to be out of danger. And keep going!"

The invisible men began running away.

Doc Savage did not follow, but raced back and began throwing the litter off the track. He slammed metal bars against the third rail that ordinarily conducted the electric power; but nothing happened. Current had not yet been turned on, and the approaching train was either motorized or carried its own batteries.

The roaring of the train increased. Doc was already moving faster than he could recall ever having moved before. But there was a great quantity of stuff on the tracks.

The train's headlight spouted whitely. The train did not slacken speed, the motorman evidently failing at first to distinguish the crowbars and pipes which composed most of the array on the rails. Then he slammed on the brakes.

A tremendous shrieking of wheels on rails filled the tunnel. Doc Savage saw he could not clear the stuff away in time, and gave it up. He sprinted madly, reached the hole which led to the tunnel through which the invisible men had come, and dived inside.

The train moaned past. The bronze man scrambled with wild haste.

Came a great crashing and rending from the tunnel.

WHAT happened was a brand of justice, if harsh. The motorman did not quite pay with his life for not seeing the obstruction in time, but it was weeks before he left a hospital. The locomotive jumped the rails, angled sidewise, hit the row of supports between the rails and knocked these over like straws until, because the posts were anchored more solidly at the bottom than at the top, the locomotive climbed up on its rear trucks and poked its snout out through the street, overturning two motor cars and vastly exciting policemen in the cordon about the vicinity.

The following cars of the train were loaded with steel rails. They smashed forward with irresistible force. Squeezing past the locomotive, they piled crosswise of the tunnel, and due to their tremendous power, rammed through the tunnel's retaining walls.

They hit a water main. It was a main some four feet in diameter, carrying high pressure, and when it burst, a Niagara was unleashed in the tunnel. The water spouted, flooded, and since there was nowhere else for it to go, it ran down the sloping tunnel toward the river, rising more than waist deep.

Telegraph Edmunds and his invisible men heard it coming. They cried out in horror. It was doubtful if any one heard their screams, for the flood made a deafening noise.

It was even doubted in some quarters that the invisible men perished; but that doubt subsided in the course of two or three weeks, when the tunnel was finally pumped dry. The bodies, after being in the water that long, were not exactly invisible, but rather, looked somewhat like large oceany jellyfish.

Doc Savage, with a good idea of what would be found after he looked into the tunnel and saw the water spouting from the main, retreated to the basement.

Chapter 19

DEATH DEVICE

REACHING the subterranean room which held the apparatus for bringing back visibility, Doc Savage discovered the homely Monk as large as life and perfectly visible.

Monk, it appeared, had put himself through the machine. He was drawing on a pair of trousers.

"I found these in a closet," he advised, then grinned widely. "I hereby resign from the spook legion. I don't care for the life."

P. Treve Easeman and Old Bonepicker, it developed, had already been through the apparatus, and had donned clothing. Doc Savage, studying the pair, saw that Old Bonepicker was indeed the plump, jovial-looking member of the pair, in spite of his aged voice.

Doc Savage himself got into the machine. Monk threw the master switch. The sensation of what happened was somewhat blurred to the bronze man, but he was conscious of much blue light and a tingling which suffused his whole body, at times almost attaining the violence of a pain. Then he began to see his own contour.

When he left the apparatus, he was normal again, although feeling rather as if he had just experienced a violent chill which had left some fever.

He found a pair of trousers in the pile which would serve, although they terminated well above his ankles.

Ada Easeman and Russel Wray appeared. They looked shaken, but showed no signs of serious damage.

Ham followed them a moment later.

"Cops are outside!" he rapped. "I told them not to come in for a while. Looks like they're convinced now that you are not mixed up with the invisible legion."

Then he retreated.

Monk said loudly, "And now I'm gonna put the guy who invented these traps through his own mill, and see what he looks like."

The homely chemist felt about on the floor, located the unconscious chief of the invisible men, and with some grunting and straining, got the fellow into the apparatus. He stepped back and threw the switch. Instantly, there was a great hissing and crackling and a play of unearthly blue haze, interspersed with regular stabs of orange and green.

In uncanny fashion, a human figure took shape before their eyes. The master plotter who had perfected the invisibility device! At first, his features were not distinguishable. Then big ears, a tremendous nose and a small mouth took form.

"Marikan!" the dapper Ham exploded, coming in from the front of the house, where he had been scouting to make sure no invisible men remained.

Monk gulped, "But they killed Marikan!"

"Pretended to kill him, it would seem," Ham corrected. "Why—he took us out to that skunk farm knowing he was leading us into a trap! He arranged the fake killing just so we wouldn't suspect him on the long chance that we should escape!"

Monk and Ham fell silent, for Marikan was stirring, evidently having been revived by the process of being made visible again. He opened his eyes. Then he lunged upright and tried to leap out of the device.

Results were disastrous. Marikan must have been dazed still, not realizing exactly where he was. He crashed into a glass tube which was making the blue haze, and it broke explosively. Hot electric sparks showered. Marikan screamed, fell backward. His body crashed into high-frequency current conductors and mashed them together, and there were more ripping sparks and showering glass.

Doc Savage dived for the switch. But it had happened too quickly. A cloud of smoke and the tang of ozone were rising from the apparatus. Doc turned the current off and ran over, along with Monk and the others.

Monk surveyed the wreckage, the lifeless body of Marikan, and shook his small head slowly.

"That guy sure took all of his secrets with him," he said.

Monk's words proved a true prediction, for in the ensuing weeks, Doc Savage conducted numerous experiments to ascertain the secret of invisibility, but with results which were scarcely phenomenal. Marikan, he concluded, had worked along some line as yet entirely unfamiliar to modern scientists.

"The mystery will have to die with Marikan," the bronze man stated. "How he did it is beyond my knowledge."

This statement was, in a sense, hardly the truth, because Doc Savage, in the course of his investigation, did come upon certain clues which told along what lines Marikan had experimented to accomplish his results. These clues, Doc believed, could be developed by himself to accomplish the same thing that Marikan had succeeded in attaining.

But he did not proceed. The process was complex. Ordinary scientists would not stumble on it, perhaps for centuries. And, judging from what had already happened, it was a thing better left alone.

There were other matters to occupy the bronze man's attention. In Marikan's discarded clothes they found a listing of the spots where the loot of the invisible men had been cached, and, thanks to that list, practically all was recovered.

There was also a matter that occupied the homely Monk's attention in the days immediately following the smashing of the menace of the invisible legion. The matter was pretty Ada Easeman. Monk pursued her industriously. It was something of a shock to him when, two days later, she announced her engagement to Russel Wray.

Monk told Habeas Corpus confidentially of the only explanation he could see.

"I was handicapped by being a spook for a while." he grumbled. "Who ever heard of a spook with a lady friend?"